THE NAUGHTIEST GIRL IS A MONITOR

Also available from Hodder Children's Books

The Naughtiest Girl in the School
The Naughtiest Girl Again
Here's the Naughtiest Girl!

The Naughtiest Girl is a Monitor

by

Enid Blyton

Illustrated by Max Schindler

a division of Hodder Headline

First published in Great Britain in 1945
This millennium edition published in 2000
by Hodder Children's Books

For further information on Enid Blyton please contact
www.blyton.com

10 9 8 7 6 5 4 3 2 1

A Catalogue record for this book is available from
the British Library

ISBN 0 340 77322 7

Typeset by Hewer Text Ltd, Edinburgh
Printed and bound in Belgium

Hodder Children's Books
a division of Hodder Headline Limited
338 Euston Road
London NW1 3BH

CHAPTER ONE

Arabella comes to stay

IT WAS in the middle of the Christmas holidays that Mother sprang a surprise on Elizabeth. Christmas was over, and Elizabeth had been to the pantomime and the circus, and to three parties.

Now she was beginning to look forward to going back to boarding-school again. It was dull being an only child, now that she had got used to living with so many girls and boys at Whyteleafe School. She missed their laughter and their chatter, the fun and games they had together.

'Mother, I love being at home – but I do miss Kathleen, Belinda, Nora and Harry and John and Richard,' she said. 'Joan has been over here to see me once or twice, but she's got a cousin staying with her now, and I don't expect I'll see her any more these hols.'

Then Mother gave Elizabeth a surprise.

'Well,' she said, 'I knew you would be lonely – so I have arranged for someone to come and keep you company for the last two weeks of these holidays, Elizabeth.'

'Mother! Who?' cried Elizabeth. 'Somebody I know?'

'No,' said Mother. 'It is a girl who is to go to Whyteleafe

School next term – a girl called Arabella Buckley. I am sure you will like her.'

'Tell me about her,' said Elizabeth, still very surprised. 'Why didn't you tell me this before, Mother?'

'Well, it has been decided in a hurry,' said Mother. 'You know Mrs Peters, don't you? She has a sister who has to go to America, and she does not want to take Arabella with her. So she wanted to put the child into a boarding-school for a year, perhaps longer.'

'And she chose Whyteleafe School!' said Elizabeth. 'Well, it's the best school in the world, *I* think!'

'That's what I told Mrs Peters,' said Mother. 'And she told her sister – and Mrs Buckley at once went to see the headmistresses, Miss Belle and Miss Best . . .'

'The Beauty and the Beast,' said Elizabeth with a grin.

'And it was arranged that Arabella should go to Whyteleafe this term,' went on Mother. 'As Mrs Buckley had to leave for America almost at once, I offered to have Arabella here – partly as company for you, and partly so that you might be able to tell her a little about Whyteleafe.'

'Mother, I do hope she's a nice sort of girl,' said Elizabeth. 'It will be fun sharing hols with someone I like, but awful if it's someone I don't like.'

'I have seen Arabella,' said Mother. 'She was a very pretty girl with most beautiful manners and she was dressed very nicely too.'

'Oh,' said Elizabeth, who was often untidily dressed, and was sometimes too impatient to have very good manners. 'Mother – I don't think I like the sound of her *very* much. Usually beautifully dressed girls aren't much good at games and things like that.'

'Well – you'll see,' said Mother. 'Anyway, she is coming tomorrow – so give her a good welcome and tell her as much about Whyteleafe as you can. I am sure she will love it.'

Elizabeth couldn't help looking forward to Arabella coming, even if she did sound rather goody-goody. She put flowers into the room her new friend was to have, and put beside the bed some of her own favourite books.

'It will be rather fun to tell someone all about Whyteleafe School,' she thought. 'I'm so proud of Whyteleafe. I think it's marvellous. And oh – I'm to be a *monitor* next term!'

Impatient, hot-tempered Elizabeth had actually been chosen to be a monitor for the coming term. It had been a great surprise to her, and she had been happier about that than about anything else in her life. She had often thought about it in the holidays, and planned how good and trustworthy and wise she would be next term.

'No quarrels with anyone – no bad tempers – no silly flare-ups!' said Elizabeth to herself. She knew her own faults very well. Indeed, all the children at Whyteleafe knew their faults, for it was part of the rule of the school that every child should be helped with his faults – and how could anyone be helped if his faults were not known?

The next day Elizabeth watched from the window for

Arabella to come. In the afternoon a rather grand car drew up at the front door. The chauffeur got out and opened the car door – and out stepped someone who looked more like a little princess than a school-girl!

'Golly!' said Elizabeth to herself, and looked down at her own plain dress of navy blue with its yellow trim. 'Golly! I shall never be able to live up to Arabella!'

Arabella was dressed in a beautiful blue coat with a white fur collar. She wore white fur gloves and a round white fur hat on her fair curls. Her eyes were very blue indeed and had dark lashes that curled up. She had a rather haughty look on her pink and white face as she stepped out of the car.

She looked at Elizabeth's house as if she didn't like it very much. The chauffeur rang the bell, and put a trunk and a bag down on the step.

Elizabeth had meant to rush down and give Arabella a hearty welcome. She had decided to call her 'Bella' because she thought Arabella rather a stupid name – 'like a doll's name,' thought Elizabeth. But somehow she didn't feel like calling her 'Bella' now.

'Arabella suits her better after all,' thought Elizabeth. 'She *is* rather like a doll with her golden curls and blue eyes, and lovely coat and hat. I don't think I like her. In fact – I think I feel a bit afraid of her!'

This was strange, because Elizabeth was rarely afraid of anything or anyone. But she had never before met anyone quite like Arabella Buckley.

'Although she's not much older than I am, she looks rather grown-up, and she walks like a grown-up – all proper – and I'm sure she talks like a grown-up too!' thought Elizabeth. 'Oh dear, I don't want to go down and talk to her.'

So she didn't go down. The maid opened the door – and then Mrs Allen, Elizabeth's mother, came hurrying forward to welcome the visitor.

She kissed Arabella, and asked her if she had had a tiring journey.

'Oh no, thank you,' said Arabella, in a clear, smooth voice. 'Our car is very comfortable, and I had plenty of sandwiches to eat halfway here. It is so kind of you to have me here, Mrs Allen. I hear you have a girl about my age.'

'Yes,' said Mrs Allen. 'She ought to be down here giving you a welcome. She said she would be. Elizabeth! Elizabeth, where are you? Arabella is here.'

So Elizabeth had to go down. She ran down the stairs in her usual manner, two at a time, landing with a bump at the bottom. She held out her hand to Arabella, who seemed a little surprised at her very sudden appearance.

'Do come down the stairs properly,' said Mrs Allen. It was a thing she said at least twelve times a day. Elizabeth never seemed able to remember to go anywhere quietly. Mrs Allen hoped that this nice, well-mannered Arabella would teach Elizabeth some of her own quietness and politeness.

'Hallo,' said Elizabeth, and Arabella held out a limp hand for her to shake.

'Good afternoon,' she said. 'How do you do?'

'Gracious!' thought Elizabeth, 'I feel as if she's Princess High-and-Mighty come to pay a call on one of her poor subjects. In a minute she'll be offering me a bowl of hot soup or a warm shawl.'

Still – it might be that Arabella was only feeling shy. Some people did go all stiff and proper when they felt shy. Elizabeth thought she had better give Arabella a chance before making up her mind about her.

'After all, I'm always making up my mind about people – and then having to unmake it because I am wrong,' thought the little girl. 'I've made an awful lot of mistakes about people at Whyteleafe School in the last two terms. I'll be careful now.'

So she smiled at Arabella and took her up to her room to wash and have a talk.

'I expect you didn't like saying goodbye to your mother, when she went off to America,' said Elizabeth in a pleasant voice. 'That was bad luck. But it's good luck for you to be going to Whyteleafe School. I can tell you that!'

'I shall be able to judge whether it is or not when I get there,' said Arabella. 'I hope to goodness there are decent children there.'

'Of course there are – and if they are horrid when they first come, we soon make them all right,' said Elizabeth. 'We had one or two boys who were awful – but now they are my best friends.'

'Boys! Did you say *boys*!' said Arabella in the greatest horror. 'I thought this was a girls' school I was going to. I hate boys!'

'It's a mixed school – boys and girls together,' said Elizabeth. 'It's fun. You won't hate boys after a bit. You soon get used to them.'

'If my mother had known there were boys at the school, I am sure she would not have sent me,' said Arabella in a tight, prim voice. 'Rough, ill-mannered creatures – dirty and untidy, with shouting voices!'

'Oh, well – even the girls get dirty and untidy sometimes,' said Elizabeth patiently, 'and as for shouting – you should just hear *me* when I'm watching a school match!'

'It sounds a terrible school to me,' said Arabella. 'I had hoped Mother would send me to Grey Towers, where two of my friends had gone – it's such a nice school. They all have their own pretty bedrooms – and wonderful food. In fact, the girls are treated like princesses.'

'Well – if you think you'll be treated like a princess at Whyteleafe, you'll jolly well find out you're wrong!' said Elizabeth sharply. 'You'll be treated as what you are – a little girl like me, with lots of things to learn! And if you put on any airs there, you'll soon be sorry, let me tell you that, Miss High-and-Mighty!'

'I think you are very rude, considering that I am a visitor, and have only just come,' said Arabella, looking down her nose in a way that made Elizabeth feel very angry. 'If that's the sort of manners they teach you at Whyteleafe, I am quite sure I shan't want to stay there more than a term.'

'I jolly well hope you don't stay a week!' said hot-tempered Elizabeth at once. She was sorry the moment after.

'Oh dear!' she said to herself. 'What a bad beginning! I really must be careful!'

CHAPTER TWO

Off to Whyteleafe School again

ARABELLA and Elizabeth did not mix well at all. There was nothing that Elizabeth liked about Arabella, and it seemed that Elizabeth was everything that Arabella most despised and hated.

Unfortunately Mother liked Arabella – and certainly the little girl had most beautiful manners. She always stood up when Mrs Allen came into the room, she opened and shut the door for her, and fetched and carried for her in a very kind and polite manner.

The politer Arabella was, the noisier Elizabeth became. And then Mrs Allen began to say things that made Elizabeth cross.

'If only you had as nice manners as Arabella, dear! I do wish you would come into a room more quietly! And I wish you would wait till I have finished speaking before you interrupt . . .'

All this made Elizabeth rather sulky. Arabella saw it, and in her smooth, polite way, she enjoyed making the differences between her and Elizabeth show up very clearly.

A week went by. Everyone in the house by this time liked Arabella, even Mrs Jenks, the rather fierce cook.

'She only likes you because you suck up to her,' said Elizabeth, when Arabella came up from the kitchen to say that Mrs Jenks was making her very favourite cake for her that afternoon.

'I don't suck up to her,' said Arabella in her usual polite tones. 'And I do wish, Elizabeth, that you wouldn't use such unladylike words. *Suck up!* I think it's a very ugly saying.'

'Oh, shut up,' said Elizabeth rudely.

Arabella sighed. 'I wish I wasn't going to Whyteleafe. If you're the sort of girl they have there, I'm not going to like it at all.'

Elizabeth sat up. 'Look here, Arabella,' she said. 'I'm just going to tell you a bit about my school, then you'll know exactly what you're in for. You *won't* like it – and the school won't like you. So it's only fair to prepare you a bit, so that you don't feel too awful when you get there.'

'All right. Tell me,' said Arabella, looking rather scared.

'Well, what I'm going to tell you would please most children,' said Elizabeth. 'It's all so sensible and fair and kind. But I dare say a Miss High-and-Mighty like you will think it's all dreadful.'

'Don't call me that,' said Arabella crossly.

'Well, listen! At Whyteleafe we have a head-boy and a head-girl. They are called William and Rita, and they are fine,' said Elizabeth. 'Then there are twelve monitors.'

'Whatever are they?' asked Arabella, wrinkling up her nose as if monitors had a nasty smell.

'They are boys and girls chosen by the whole school as leaders,' said Elizabeth. 'They are chosen because we trust them, and know them to be kind and just and wise. They see that we keep the rules, they keep the rules themselves, and they help Rita and William to decide what punishments and rewards the children must have at each Weekly Meeting.'

'What's the Weekly Meeting?' asked Arabella, her blue eyes round with surprise.

'It's a kind of School Parliament,' said Elizabeth, enjoying telling Arabella all these things. 'At each meeting we put into the money-box any money we have had that week – that's the rule . . .'

'What! Put our own money into a school money-box!' said Arabella in horror. 'I have a lot of money. *I* shan't do that! What a mad idea.'

'It seems mad at first if you're not used to it,' said Elizabeth, remembering how she had hated the idea two terms ago. 'But actually it's a very good idea. You see, Arabella, it doesn't do for one or two of us to have pounds and pounds to spend at school – and the rest of us only a few. That's not fair.'

'I think it's quite fair,' said Arabella, knowing that she would be one of the few very rich ones.

'Well, it isn't,' said Elizabeth. 'What we do is – we all put our money in, and then we are each given two pounds out of the box, to spend as we like. So we all have the same.'

'Only two pounds!' said Arabella, looking quite horrified.

'Well, if you badly want some more, you have to tell the head-boy and girl, and they will decide whether you can have it or not,' said Elizabeth.

'What else do you do at the Meeting?' asked Arabella. 'I think it all sounds dreadful. Don't the headmistresses have a say in anything?'

'Only if we ask them,' said Elizabeth. 'You see, they like us to make our own rules, plan our own punishments, and give our own rewards. For instance, Arabella, suppose you were too high-and-mighty for anything, well, we would try to cure you by—'

'You won't try to cure me of anything,' said Arabella in a very stiff tone. 'You're the one that ought to be cured of a lot of things. I wonder the monitors haven't tried to cure you before now. Perhaps they will this term.'

'I've been chosen to *be* a monitor,' said Elizabeth proudly. 'I shall be one of the twelve jurymen, sitting up on the platform. If a complaint is made about *you* by anyone, I shall have power to judge it and say what ought to be done with you.'

Arabella went very red. 'The very idea of a tomboy like you judging *me*!' she said. 'You don't know how to walk properly, you don't know your manners, and you laugh much too loudly.'

'Oh, be quiet,' said Elizabeth. 'I'm not prim and proper like you. I don't suck up to every grown-up I meet. I don't pretend, and put on airs and graces and try to look like a silly, beautifully dressed doll who says Ma-ma when you pull a string!'

'Elizabeth Allen, if I were like you, I'd throw something at your head for saying that!' said Arabella, standing up in a rage.

'Well, throw it, then,' said Elizabeth. 'Anything would be better than being such a good-little-girl, Mummy's-precious-darling!'

Arabella went out of the room, and so far forgot her manners as to slam the door, a thing she had never done in her life before. Elizabeth grinned. Then she looked thoughtful.

'Now,' she said to herself, 'you be careful, Elizabeth Allen. You're very good at making enemies, but you know quite well that leads to nothing but rows and unhappiness. Arabella's an idiot – a conceited, silly, empty-headed doll – you let Whyteleafe deal with her, and don't try to cure her all at once by yourself. Try to be friends and help her.'

So Elizabeth tried to forget how much she disliked vain little Arabella and her doll-like clothes and manners, and treated her in as friendly a manner as she could. But she was very glad indeed when the day came for her to return to school. It was dreadful to have no other companion but Arabella. At Whyteleafe she would have dozens of others round her, all talking and laughing. She need never speak to Arabella unless she wanted to.

'She's older than I am, and perhaps she will be in a higher form,' she thought, as she put on her school uniform with delight. It was a nice uniform. The coat was dark blue with a yellow edge to the collar and cuffs. The hat was also dark blue, and had a yellow band. On her legs Elizabeth wore long brown stockings, and brown laced shoes on her feet.

'How I hate these dark school clothes,' said Arabella in disgust. 'What a dreadful uniform! Now at Grey Towers, the school I wanted to go to, the girls are allowed to wear anything that suits them.'

'How silly,' said Elizabeth. She looked at Arabella. The girl seemed different now that she was in the ordinary school uniform, and not in her expensive, well-cut clothes. She looked more like a school-girl and less like a pink-faced doll.

'I like you better in your uniform,' said Elizabeth. 'You look more real, somehow.'

'Elizabeth, you do say extraordinary things,' said Arabella in surprise. 'I'm as real as you are.'

'I don't think you are,' said Elizabeth, looking hard at Arabella. 'You're all hidden away behind airs and graces, and good manners and sweet speeches, and I don't know if there is a real You at all!'

'I think you're silly,' said Arabella.

'Girls! Are you ready!' called Mrs Allen. 'The car is at the door.'

They went downstairs, carrying their small night-bags.

Each girl had to take a small bag with the things in it that she would need for the first night, such as a nightdress, toothbrush and so on, for their big trunks were not unpacked till the next day.

They carried lacrosse and hockey-sticks, though Arabella had said she hoped she wouldn't have to play either game. She hated games.

They caught the train up to London, and at the big station there they met the girls and boys returning to their school. Miss Ranger, Elizabeth's form-mistress, was there, and she welcomed Elizabeth.

'This is Arabella Buckley,' said Elizabeth. All the boys and girls turned round to look at Arabella. How new and spick and span she looked. Not a hair out of place, no wrinkles in her brown stockings, no smut on her cheek!

'Hallo, Elizabeth!' cried Joan, and put her arm through her friend's.

'Hallo, Elizabeth! Hallo, Elizabeth!'

One by one all her friends came up, smiling, delighted to see the girl who had once been the naughtiest in the school. Harry clapped her on the back and so did Robert. John asked her if she had done any gardening. Kathleen came up, rosy-cheeked and dimpled. Richard waved to her as he carried a violin-case to the train.

'Oh, it's lovely to be back with them all again,' thought Elizabeth. 'And this term – this term I'm to be a monitor! And won't I be a success! I'll make that stuck-up Arabella look up to me all right!'

'Get in the train quickly!' called Miss Ranger. 'Say goodbye, and get in.'

The guard blew his whistle. The train puffed out. They were off to Whyteleafe once more.

CHAPTER THREE

Four new children

ONE OF the exciting things about a new term is – are there any new children? What are they like? Whose form will they be in?

All the old children looked to see who was new. Arabella was, of course. Then there were three more, two of them boys, and one a girl.

Elizabeth, as a monitor, made it her business to make the new children feel at home. As soon as they arrived at Whyteleafe she set things going.

'Kathleen, show Arabella her dormitory, and tell her the rules. I'll help the other three. Robert, will you give a hand too? You will have two new boys to see to today.'

'Right,' said Robert, grinning. He had grown in the holidays and was tall and burly now. He was glad to be back at school, for at Whyteleafe were the horses he loved so much. He hoped that he would be allowed to take charge of some of them, as he had been the term before.

Elizabeth turned to the new children. Arabella had already gone off with Kathleen, looking rather scared. The other three new ones stood together, one boy making rather a curious noise, like a hen clucking.

'That's just like a hen clucking,' said Elizabeth. 'You sound as if you've laid an egg!'

The boy grinned. 'I can imitate most animals,' he said. 'My name's Julian Holland. What's yours?'

'Elizabeth Allen,' said Elizabeth. She looked at the new boy with interest. He was the untidiest person she had ever seen. He had long black hair that fell in a wild lock over his forehead, and his eyes were deep green, and brilliant, like a cat's. 'He looks jolly clever,' said Elizabeth to herself. 'I bet he'll be top of the class if he's with Miss Ranger.'

The boy made a noise like a turkey gobbling. Mr Lewis, the music-master, was passing by, and looked round, startled. Julian at once made a noise like a violin being tuned, which made Mr Lewis hurry into the nearest music-practice room, thinking that someone must be there with a violin.

Elizabeth gave a squeal of laughter. 'Oh! You *are* clever! I hope you're in my form.'

The other boy, Martin, was quite different. He looked very clean and neat and tidy. His hair was well-brushed back from his forehead, and his eyes were a very clear blue. They were set a little close together, but they had a very wide and innocent expression. Elizabeth liked him.

'I'm Martin Follett,' he said in a pleasant voice.

'And I'm Rosemary Wing,' said the new girl, rather shyly. She had a pretty little face, with a smiling mouth, but her eyes were rather small, and she did not seem to like to look anyone full in the face. Elizabeth thought she must feel very shy. Well, she would soon get over that.

'Robert, you take Julian and Martin to the boys' dormitories,' she said, 'and I'll take Rosemary to hers. Hang on to them till they know their way about, won't you, and show them where they have their meals and things like that.'

'Right, Monitor,' said Robert, with another grin. Elizabeth felt proud. It was grand to be a monitor.

'Oh, are you a monitor?' asked Rosemary, trotting after Elizabeth. 'That's something very special, isn't it?'

'It is rather,' said Elizabeth. 'I'm *your* monitor, Rosemary. So, if ever you are in any difficulty or trouble, you must come to me and tell me – and I'll try and help you.'

'I thought we had to bring our troubles or complaints to the Weekly Meeting,' said Rosemary. She had heard about this in the train that day.

'Oh yes; but at first you had better tell *me* what you'd like to bring before the Meeting,' said Elizabeth, 'because, you see, we are only allowed to bring *proper* difficulties or complaints to the Meeting – not just tales. You might not know the difference between just telling tales and bringing a real complaint.'

'I see,' said Rosemary. 'That's a very good idea. I'll do that.'

'She's a nice little thing,' thought Elizabeth, as she showed Rosemary where to put her things and told her to put out her toothbrush, hair-brush and nightdress. 'By the way, Rosemary, we are only allowed to have six things out on our dressing-tables, not more. You can choose what you like.'

It was fun to give out the rules like this. Elizabeth remembered how Nora, her own monitor two terms ago, had told *her* the rules – and how she had disobeyed them at once by putting out eleven things! She wondered now how she could have been so silly – how she could have dared!

'Yes, Elizabeth,' said Rosemary obediently and she counted the things to put out.

In the next dormitory Kathleen was having trouble with Arabella, who was very scornful about all the rules told her.

'Well, there are not many,' said Kathleen, 'and after all, we make the rules ourselves, so we ought to obey them, Arabella. I'll fetch Elizabeth here, if you like – she is the monitor and can tell you the rules properly.'

'I don't want to see Elizabeth,' said Arabella at once. 'I saw her quite enough in the holidays. I only hope I'm not in the same form.'

Kathleen had a great admiration for Elizabeth, although she had hated her part of the term before. She spoke up at once.

'You'd better not say things like that about our monitors. We choose them ourselves because we like and admire them. Anyway, it's bad manners to talk like that about somebody whose guest you have just been.'

Arabella had never in her life been accused of bad manners before. She went quite pale and could think of nothing to say. She looked at Kathleen and decided that she didn't like her. In fact, she didn't think she liked anyone at all, so far, except that little pretty girl called Rosemary – the one who was new. Perhaps she could make friends with her. Arabella felt sure that Rosemary would be most impressed with her tales of wealth, rich clothes, and marvellous holidays.

The next few days everyone settled down. A few were homesick, but Whyteleafe was such a sensible school and the children were so jolly and friendly that even new boys and girls found it hard to miss their homes. There was laughter and chatter to be heard everywhere.

All the new children were in Elizabeth's class. Good! It was fun to have new children, and now that Elizabeth was a monitor, it was nice to impress Julian and the others. Joan had gone up into the next class, so Elizabeth was the only monitor in hers.

Miss Ranger, the form-mistress, soon sized up the new children, and talked them over with Mam'zelle.

'Julian is a lazy boy,' she said. 'A pity, because I'm sure he has a wonderful brain. He thinks of plenty of clever things to do *outside* lessons. He can make simply anything with his hands. I saw him showing the others a little aeroplane he had made – it flies beautifully. All his own ideas are in it, none of them copied. He'll spend hours thinking out things like that – but not one minute will he spend on learning his geography or history!'

'Ah, that Julian,' said Mam'zelle, in a tone of great disgust. 'I do not like him. Always he makes some extraordinary noise.'

'Noise?' said Miss Ranger in surprise. 'Well, I must say he hasn't tried out any extraordinary noises on me yet. But I dare say he will.'

'Yesterday, in my class, there was a noise like a lost kitten,' said Mam'zelle. 'Ah, the poor thing!' I said. 'It has come into our big classroom and got lost. And for ten minutes I looked for it. But it was that boy Julian doing his mews.'

'Really?' said Miss Ranger, making up her mind that Julian would not do any mews or barks or whines in *her* class. 'Well, thanks for the tip. I'll look out for Julian's noises!'

The talk passed on to Arabella. 'A silly, empty-headed doll,' said Miss Ranger. 'I hope we can make something out of her. She really ought to be in the next class, but she is rather backward, so I must push her on a bit before she goes up. She seems to have a very high opinion of herself! She is always doing her hair or smoothing down her dress – or else trying to show us what perfect manners she has!'

'She is not bad, that one,' said Mam'zelle, who was quite pleased with Arabella because the girl had lived for a year in France and could speak French well. 'In my country, Miss Ranger, the children have better manners than the children here – and it is pleasant to see one with manners as good as Arabella's.'

'Hm,' said Miss Ranger, who knew that Mam'zelle would rarely have anything to say against children who spoke French well. 'What do you think of Martin – and Rosemary?'

'Oh, the sweet children!' said Mam'zelle, who loved Rosemary's willingness to please, and to obey her in everything. 'The little Martin now – he is so good, he tries so hard.'

'Well, I'm not so sure about him,' said Miss Ranger. 'Rosemary is all right, I think – but she's a weak little thing. I hope she'll make the right friends. I wish Elizabeth Allen or Jenny would make friends with her.'

So the teachers sized up their new children – and the old children sized them up too. Julian was an enormous success. He was a real dare-devil, with most extraordinary gifts which he used when he pleased. He had a wonderful brain, inventive and brilliant, and he could make all kinds of things, and think of all kinds of amusing tricks which he was quite prepared to perform in class as soon as he had settled down a bit.

'It's a shame you are so low in form, Julian,' said Elizabeth at the end of a week. 'You've got such marvellous brains. You ought to be top!'

Julian looked at her with his brilliant green eyes. 'Can't be bothered,' he said in his slow, deep voice. 'Who wants to learn history dates? I'll forget them all when I'm grown. Who wants to learn the highest mountains in the world? I'll never climb them, so I don't care. Lessons are a bore.'

Elizabeth remembered that she was a monitor. She spoke earnestly to Julian.

'Julian, do work hard. Do try to be top.'

Julian laughed. 'You're just saying that because you've remembered you're a monitor! You can't catch *me* with goody-goody talk like that! You'll have to think of some jolly good reason for me to work hard before I do!'

Elizabeth went red. She didn't like being called goody-goody. She turned away.

But Julian came after her. 'It's all right, I'm only teasing,' he said. 'Listen, Elizabeth – Joan, your best friend, has gone up into the next form – so why can't *we* be friends? You've got the best brain in the form – after mine, of course – and you're fun. You be my friend.'

'All right,' said Elizabeth, rather proud that the brilliant and unusual Julian should ask her. 'All right. We'll be friends. It will be fun.'

It *was* fun – but it brought a lot of trouble too!

CHAPTER FOUR

The School Meeting

ARABELLA AND the other new children waited with much interest for the first Meeting. At none of their other schools had they had a kind of school Parliament, run by the children themselves. They wondered what it would be like.

'It sounds a good idea,' said Martin.

'I think so too,' said Rosemary, in her timid little voice. She always agreed with everyone, no matter what they said.

'Stupid idea, *I* think,' said Arabella. She made a point of running down everything at Whyteleafe if she could, because she had so badly wanted to go to the grand school her friends had gone to – and she looked down on Whyteleafe, with its sensible ideas.

Julian unexpectedly agreed with her, though he usually had no time for Arabella, with her silly airs and graces. 'I can't say *I* shall bother much about the School Meeting,' he said. 'I don't care what it says or does. It will never make any difference to me. As long as I can do what I like I am quite willing to let others do what *they* like too.'

'Oh, Julian – you say that, but you don't mean it,' said Kathleen. 'You'd hate it if someone broke one of the things you are always making, you know! Or told tales about you, or something like that. You'd go up in smoke!'

Julian did not like being argued with. He tossed his long black hair back, and screwed up his nose in the way he always did when he was annoyed. He was making a tiny boat out of an odd bit of wood. It was like magic to see it form under his hand.

'Anyone can tell tales of me as much as they like!' said Julian. 'I don't care about anything so long as I can do what I like.'

'You're a funny boy, I think,' said Jenny. 'You are either terribly stupid in class, or – just sometimes – terribly bright.'

'Why? What did he do that was so bright?' asked Joan, who was listening. She was in the next form, and so did not see Julian in class.

'We were having mental arithmetic,' said Jenny. 'And usually Julian gets every single thing wrong in maths. Well, for some reason or other – just because he wanted to show off, I think – he answered every single question right, straight off, almost before Miss Ranger had got them out of her mouth!'

'Yes, and Miss Ranger was so astonished,' said Belinda. 'She went on asking him harder and harder ones – things *we* would have to think about and work out in our heads for a minute or two – but Julian just answered them pat. It was funny.'

'It made Miss Ranger awfully cross with him next time,

though,' said Kathleen, 'because at the next maths lesson, he seemed to go to sleep and wouldn't answer a thing.'

Julian grinned. He really was an extraordinary boy. The others couldn't help liking him. He was so exciting. They all begged and begged him to make some of his amazing noises in Miss Ranger's class, but he wouldn't.

'She's watching out for them, I know she is,' he said. 'It's no fun doing them if people know it's me. It's *really* fun when people honestly think there's a kitten in the room – or something like that – like Mam'zelle did the other day. You wait. I'll give you some fun one day soon – but I'd like to choose the person myself to try my tricks on.'

Elizabeth was longing for the first School Meeting. She wanted to go and sit up on the platform with the other monitors, in front of the whole school. She was not vain about being made a monitor, but she was rightly proud of it.

'It really is an honour,' she said to herself. 'It does mean that the school trusts me and thinks I'm worthwhile. Oh, I do hope this term will go well, without any upsets or troubles.'

The children filed into the big hall for the first Meeting. Then in came the twelve monitors, serious-faced. They took their places, and sat, like a thoughtful jury, in front of all the children. Arabella gazed at Elizabeth with dislike. Fancy that tomboy, with her bad manners, being made a monitor!

Then in came William and Rita, the head-boy and girl,

the Judges of the whole Meeting. All the children rose to their feet as they came in.

At the back sat Miss Belle and Miss Best, the two headmistresses, with Mr Johns, one of the masters. They were always interested in the Meetings, but unless the head-boy and girl asked them to, they did not enter into it in any way. This was the children's own Parliament, where they made their own laws, their own rules, and where they themselves rewarded or punished any child who deserved it.

There was very little to talk about at that first Meeting. Every child was told to put what money it had into the big school money-box. Elizabeth looked with interest at Arabella, when she was sent round with the Box. Would Arabella refuse to put in her money?

Arabella sat looking as if butter would not melt in her mouth. When the box came to her, she put in a ten-pound note and two separate pound coins. She did not look at Elizabeth.

Most of the children had quite a lot of money to put into the Box at the beginning of term. Parents, uncles, and aunts had given them pounds, pennies, and even notes to go back to school with, and the box felt nice and heavy when Elizabeth took it back to William and Rita.

'Thank you,' said William. The children were all talking together, and William knocked on the table with his little hammer. At once there was silence – except for a curious bubbling noise, like a saucepan boiling over.

It seemed to come from somewhere near Jenny, Julian and Kathleen. William looked rather astonished. He knocked again with his hammer – but still the noise went on, a little louder, if anything.

Elizabeth knew at once that it was one of Julian's extraordinary noises. She looked at him. He sat on the form, his green eyes looking over the heads of the others, his mouth and throat perfectly still. How *could* he do noises like that? Elizabeth felt a tremendous giggle coming and she swallowed it down quickly.

'I mustn't giggle when I'm sitting up here as monitor,' she thought. 'Oh dear, I wish Julian would stop. It's just like a saucepan boiling over, but louder.'

By this time one or two children were giggling, and William knocked sharply with his hammer again. Elizabeth wondered if she ought to say that it was Julian who was making the noise and holding up the Meeting.

'But I can't. He's my friend. And I'm not going to get him into trouble, even if I *am* a monitor,' she thought. She tried to make Julian look at her, and he suddenly did. She glared at him, then frowned.

Julian made one last loud bubbling noise, and then stopped. William had no idea at all who had made the noise. He gazed round the Meeting.

'It may be funny to hold up the School Meeting *once*,' he said. 'But it would not be funny a second time. We will now get on with the money-sharing.'

Each child came up to take two pounds from the

monitors, out of the School Box. William had brought plenty of change with him, which he put into the Box, taking out the notes instead.

When each child had their two pounds for spending, William spoke again.

'The new children probably know that out of this two pounds they must buy their own stamps, sweets, hair-ribbons, papers, and so on that they want. If any extra money is needed, it can be asked for. Does anyone want any extra this week?'

John Terry stood up. He was in charge of the school garden, and was a very hard and very good worker. He, with those other children who helped him, managed to supply the school with fine vegetables and flowers. Everyone was proud of John.

'William, we could do with a new small barrow,' he said. 'You see, there are one or two of the younger children who are helping in the garden this term, and the old barrow is really too heavy for them.'

'Well, how much would a smaller one cost?' asked William. 'We've got plenty of money in the Box at the moment, but we don't want to spend too much money.'

John Terry had a price-list with him. He read out the prices of various barrows.

'They seem very expensive,' said William. 'I almost think we had better wait a bit to see if the younger children are going to go on being keen, John. You know what sometimes happens – they start so well, and then get tired of it. It would be a waste of a barrow if we bought it and then no one used it.'

John looked disappointed. 'Well,' he said, 'it's just as you like, William. But I do think the youngsters are keen. Peter is, anyway. He worked hard last term, and I really couldn't do without him in the garden now. He's got his two friends with him now, helping us.'

Small Peter glowed red with pleasure at hearing John say this. His two small friends at once made up their minds that they would work hard in the garden too, and make John as proud of them as he seemed to be of Peter.

'Has anyone anything to say about a new barrow?' asked Rita. Nobody spoke – until Julian suddenly opened his mouth and spoke in his deep voice.

'Yes. Let the youngsters have their barrow – but I'll make it for them. I can easily do that.'

Julian had not stood up to speak. He lolled on the form in his usual lazy fashion.

'Stand up when you speak,' said Rita. Julian looked as if he was not going to. But at last he did, and then repeated his offer.

'I'll make a barrow, a small one. If I can go into the sheds, I can easily find everything I want. You don't need to spend any money then.'

Everyone was interested. Elizabeth spoke up eagerly.

'Let Julian do it, William! He's awfully clever at making things. He can make *any*thing!'

'Very well. Thank you for your offer, Julian,' said

William. 'Get on with the job as soon as you can. Now – any other business to discuss?'

There was not. William closed the Meeting and the children filed out.

'Good, Julian!' said Elizabeth, slipping her arm through his. 'I bet you'll make the finest barrow in the world!'

CHAPTER FIVE

Arabella gets into trouble

ALL THE new children settled down as the days went on. Julian set about making the new barrow in a very workmanlike way. He explored the various sheds, and brought out an old rubber wheel that had once belonged to somebody's tricycle. He found some odd bits of wood and other odds and ends, and took them all to the carpentering room.

The children heard him whistling there as he hammered away. Then they heard the creaking of a barrow being wheeled up and down.

'Golly! Has he finished it already?' said Harry in surprise. 'He's a marvel!'

But he hadn't, of course. He was only making one of his noises. His green eyes twinkled as the children peeped round the door. He loved a joke.

The boys and girls crowded round him, exclaiming in admiration.

'Julian! It's going to be a marvellous barrow! Julian, how clever you are!'

'No, I'm not,' said Julian, laughing. 'I was bottom of the form this week. Didn't you hear?'

'Well, the barrow is fine, anyway,' said Belinda. 'It's just as good as a real one.'

Julian cared for neither praise nor blame. He had not offered to make the barrow because he was sorry that the youngsters hadn't one. He had offered to make it simply because he knew he could, and he would enjoy making it.

Julian was very well liked, for all his don't-care ways. But Arabella was not. She would make friends with no one but the little meek Rosemary. Rosemary thought the lovely well-mannered girl was like a princess. She followed her everywhere, listened eagerly to all she said and agreed with everything.

'I think this is a stupid school,' Arabella said to Rosemary many times. 'Think of the silly rules it has – all the sillier because they are made by the children themselves.'

Up till then Rosemary had thought that the reason the rules were so good was because they *had* been made by the boys and girls. But now she agreed with Arabella at once.

'Yes. They *are* silly.'

'Especially the one about putting all our money into the school money-box,' said Arabella.

This had not mattered much to Rosemary, who had only had two pounds and fifty pence to put in. Her parents were not very well off, and she had not been given much money at any time. Still, she agreed with Arabella, of course.

'Yes, that's a very silly rule,' she said. 'Especially for people like you, Arabella, who have to give up so much money. It's a shame. I saw you put in the ten-pound note and the two pound coins.'

Arabella looked at Rosemary and wondered if she could trust her – for Arabella had a secret. She had not put in all her money! She had kept a five-pound note for herself, so that, with the two pounds she had been allowed, she had seven pounds. She was not going to give that up for anyone! It was hidden in her handkerchief case, neatly folded up in a hanky.

'No,' she thought. 'I won't tell Rosemary yet. I don't know her very well, and although she is my friend, she's a bit silly somctimes. I'll keep my own secret.'

So she told no one. But she and Rosemary went down to the town together that day to buy stamps, and a hair-grip for Rosemary – and Arabella could not help spending some of her money!

'You go to the post-office and buy your stamps, and I'll go and buy some chocolates at the sweet-shop,' she said to Rosemary. She did not want the other girl to see her buying expensive chocolates, and handing over two or three pounds for them.

So, while Rosemary was buying a stamp in the post-office, Arabella slipped into the big sweet-shop and bought a pound of peppermint chocolates, the kind she loved.

She saw a bottle of barley-sugar too, and bought that. Lovely! Then, as Rosemary didn't come, she went into the shop next door, and bought herself a book.

The two girls wandered round the town a little while, and then went back to school. 'You know,' said Arabella, linking her arm in Rosemary's, 'you know, that's another silly Whyteleafe rule – that no one is allowed to go down to the town alone unless she's a monitor or in the higher forms.'

'Awfully silly,' agreed Rosemary. Arabella undid the bag of chocolates. 'Have one?' she said.

'Oooh, Arabella – what a lovely lot of chocolates!' said Rosemary, her rather small eyes opening wide. 'Golly, you must have spent all your two pounds at once!'

They went in at the school gate, munching chocolates. They were really delicious. Arabella shut up the bag and stuffed it into her winter coat pocket. She did not want the others to see what a lot of chocolates she had, in case they might guess she had spent more than two pounds on them.

She went to take off her hat and coat. Jenny was putting hers on, and when Arabella put the book she had bought down on the bench between them, Jenny picked it up.

'Hallo! I always wanted to read this book. Lend it to me, will you, Arabella?'

'Well, I haven't read it myself yet,' said Arabella. 'I only bought it this afternoon.'

Jenny looked at the price inside the cover, and whistled. It's a three-pound book. How could you buy that with two pounds?'

'I got it cheap,' said Arabella, after a moment's pause.

She went red as she said it, and sharp-eyed Jenny saw the blush. She said no more, but went off, thinking hard.

'The mean thing! She didn't put all her money into the box!' thought Jenny.

Rosemary annoyed Arabella very much that evening when they were in the common-room together, because she gave away the fact that Arabella had bought the chocolate peppermints! She did not mean to, of course – but she did it, all the same!

The children were talking about the sweet-shop, which they all loved, and where they all spent money each week.

'I think those boiled sweets are the best bargain,' said Jenny.

'Oh no – those clear gums last much the longest,' said Belinda.

'Not if you chew them,' said Harry. 'I bet if you sucked a boiled sweet properly, right to the end without crunching it up, and after that sucked a clear gum without chewing at all, there wouldn't be much to choose between them.'

'Let's have a competition and see,' said John.

'It's no good *me* trying,' said Jenny. 'I always crunch everything, and it goes like lightning down my throat.'

'*I* think the best bargain of all is chocolate peppermints,' suddenly said Rosemary's meek little voice.

Everyone laughed scornfully. 'Idiot!' said Julian. 'You only get about five for fifty pence. They are most awfully expensive.'

'They're not,' said Rosemary, 'really they are not.

Arabella, show them the enormous bagful you got today at the shop.'

This was the last thing that Arabella wanted to do. She frowned heavily at Rosemary.

'Don't be silly,' she said. 'I only got a few. They *are* expensive.'

Rosemary was amazed. Hadn't she taken one herself from an overflowing bag? She opened her mouth to say so, but caught sight of Arabella's warning face and stopped.

The others had listened to all this with much interest. They felt perfectly certain that Arabella had spent a lot of money on the chocolates, and Jenny remembered the book too. She looked sharply at Arabella.

But Arabella was now looking her usual calm self, rather haughty. 'You're a deceitful person, in spite of your grand, high-and-mighty ways,' thought Jenny to herself. 'I bet you've got those chocolates hidden away somewhere, so that no one shall know you spent a lot of money on them. I'll find them too – just see if I won't!'

Arabella got up in a few minutes and went out. She soon came back, carrying a small paper bag in which were six or seven chocolate peppermints. 'These are all I got for my money,' she said graciously. 'I'm afraid there isn't enough for one each – but we could divide them in half.'

But nobody wanted any. It was an unwritten rule at Whyteleafe that if you didn't like a person, you didn't accept things from them. So everyone except Rosemary said no. Rosemary took one, feeling puzzled and astonished. She *knew* she had seen a much bigger bag of chocolate peppermints before. Could she have been mistaken?

Jenny grinned to herself. Arabella must think they were all stupid if she thought she could make the other boys and girls believe she had only bought a few sweets – when that silly little Rosemary had given the secret away! She wondered where Arabella could have hidden the rest of the chocolates.

She thought she knew. Arabella learnt music and had a big music-case. Jenny had seen her go to it that afternoon, although she had neither lesson nor practice to do. Why?

'Because she wanted to put her chocs there,' thought Jenny. She slipped off to the music-room, where everyone kept their music. She took up Arabella's case and peeped inside it. The chocolate peppermints were there, where Arabella had hurriedly emptied them.

Richard came into the room whilst she was looking. 'See Richard,' said Jenny, in a tone of disgust. 'Arabella has kept some money back – and bought heaps of chocs and a book – and told all kinds of lies.'

'Well, make a complaint at the Meeting, then,' said Richard, taking up his case and going out.

Jenny stood and thought for a moment. 'Would a complaint at the Meeting be thought a tale?' she wondered. She had better ask the others before saying anything. But she wouldn't tell Elizabeth – not yet, anyhow – because Arabella had been staying with Elizabeth, and it might be awkward for the new monitor if she knew about Arabella.

So Jenny told the others, when Elizabeth, Rosemary, and Arabella were not there. They were really disgusted.

'I'm sure it would be a proper complaint,' said Harry. 'All the same, it's rather awful to have your name brought up at the Meeting quite so soon in the term, just when you're still new. Let's just show Arabella that we think her jolly mean. She'll soon guess why – and at the next Meeting I bet she'll pop *all* her money into the Box!'

Then poor Arabella was in for a bad time! For the first time in her life she knew what it was to be with children who didn't like her at all, and who showed it!

CHAPTER SIX

Arabella makes a complaint

ARABELLA HAD turned up her nose at the boys and girls of Whyteleafe School from the first day she had arrived. She had told Rosemary that she didn't care whether they liked her or whether they didn't.

But it was difficult not to mind when everyone seemed to turn up their noses at her! It gave Arabella a very important, superior sort of feeling to despise all her class except Rosemary. But it gave her quite a different kind of feeling when she felt *she* was despised!

The children would not have been so thorough about it if Arabella had not behaved so stupidly from the beginning. Now they couldn't help feeling they were getting a bit of their own back!

'They treat me as if I was a bad smell!' Arabella complained to the faithful Rosemary. 'Why, that horrid boy Julian actually holds his nose when he passes me.'

This was quite true. Julian did hold his nose with his finger and thumb every time he came near Arabella. It annoyed her dreadfully. She was so used to being looked up to and admired by children, and to being praised by grown-ups that she simply didn't understand this sort of behaviour. It made her very angry indeed.

Arabella did not guess why the children were treating her like this. She had no idea that it was because they thought she had been dishonest and deceitful over her money. She felt sure she had been so clever about that that no one knew about it. She did not know that Jenny had peeped into her music-case and seen the chocolates there.

Jenny entered into the fun of teasing Arabella too. Her way of teasing her was to talk in a very smooth, polite voice, exactly like Arabella's, of amazing riches and wonderful holidays, in the very same way that Arabella loved to talk.

Jenny was a very good mimic. She could imitate anyone's voice, and anyone's laugh. It made the children giggle to hear her talking just like Arabella, when Arabella was there.

'And, my dears,' Jenny would say, '*last* hols were the most marvellous of all. We actually took three cars with us when we went away – and the last one held nothing but my party clothes! Oh, and I really must tell you of the time when I went to stay with my grandmother. She allowed me to stay up to dinner *every* night, and we had fifteen different courses to eat, and four different sorts of – of – ginger beer!'

Shrieks of laughter followed all this. Only Arabella did not laugh. She did not think it was at all funny. She thought it was simply horrid. At her old school everyone had loved hearing her tales. Why did they make fun of them at this nasty school?

Another very annoying thing happened to Arabella, too. She would be sitting in the common-room, sewing or writing, and suddenly Jenny or someone would say 'Oh, look – is that an aeroplane?' Or, 'I say – is that a moth?' pointing at the same time out of the window or up to the ceiling.

Everyone would at once turn their heads, Arabella as well – and when poor Arabella turned back to her sewing or her writing, she would find her pen gone, or her scissors. She would hunt on the floor for them until she suddenly heard a giggle.

Then she would know that someone had quickly snatched them up and put them on the window-sill or on a desk in the corner, just to tease her.

She told Rosemary about all the teasing, and the other girl listened with sympathy. 'It's too bad, Arabella,' she said. 'I don't know why they do it.'

'Well, you ask them, and find out,' said Arabella. 'See? Now, don't forget – and don't say I asked you to find out.'

So, when Arabella was next out of the room Rosemary found courage enough to speak to Jenny.

'Why are you so beastly to Arabella?'

'Because she deserves it,' said Jenny shortly.

'Why does she deserve it?' asked Rosemary.

'Well, don't you think she's a stuck-up, deceitful creature?' said Jenny. 'I know you're always hanging round her like a little dog, but you must surely know it's dishonest to keep back money from the School Box and spend it on herself – and then tell lies about it.'

Jenny's sharp eyes were fixed on timid Rosemary. The other girl dropped her eyes and did not look at Jenny.

She was too weak to stick up for her friend, or even to say that she did not know that what Jenny said was true – though now that Jenny had said it, it did seem to Rosemary that Arabella *had* been deceitful.

'Yes. That was bad,' said Rosemary at last. 'Oh dear. Is that why you are so horrid to her?'

'Well, she must know why we are,' said Jenny impatiently. 'She's not so stupid as all that, surely.'

Rosemary did not like to say that Arabella had no idea why everyone was horrid to her. Neither did she like to tell Arabella why the others were annoying her so. She was like a leaf in the wind, blown this way and that – 'Shall I tell her? I'd better. No. I can't, she'd be angry. Well, I won't tell her then. Oh, perhaps I'd better. No, I really can't.'

So, in the end Rosemary did not tell Arabella and when Arabella asked her what the others had said, she shook her head.

'They're – they're just teasing you because they think it's fun,' she said. 'Just because they're horrid.'

'Oh!' said Arabella, red with anger. 'Well – I shall complain to the Meeting. I just won't have this happen!'

'Oh, Arabella, don't do that,' said Rosemary in alarm. 'They might say it was telling tales – and you'd get into worse trouble! Tell your monitor first, and see if she thinks it would be telling tales to tell the Meeting.'

'I certainly shan't say anything to Elizabeth!' said Arabella. 'Go and ask advice from *her*? No, thank you!'

And so silly Arabella, not guessing the trouble that would come to her, boiled away inside all the week, hating the others and longing for the Meeting to come!

It came at last. Arabella's lips were tightly pressed together as she looked round at the children of her form. 'Just wait!' her eyes seemed to say. 'Just wait and see how I will show you up!'

The School money-box was handed round, but not very much was put in. Arabella put nothing in. Then the two pounds were handed to everyone, and the usual business began.

'Any requests?'

'Please can I have fifty pence extra, William?' asked Belinda, standing up. 'A letter came for me this week without a stamp on – so I had to pay double postage on it, and it cost me fifty pence. It was from one of my aunts. I expect she forgot to put a stamp on.'

'Fifty pence for Belinda,' ordered William. 'It wasn't her fault that she had to pay extra.'

Fifty pence was handed out to Belinda, and she sat down, pleased.

'Could I have sixty pence to buy a new ball, please?' said a small boy, standing up rather shyly. 'Mine rolled down the railway bank and we're not allowed to go on the line.'

'Go to Eileen, and she will sell you one of our old balls for twenty pence,' said William. 'You will have to pay it out of your own money.'

There were no more requests. The children were whispering between themselves and William knocked on his table with his little hammer. Everyone stopped talking.

'Any complaints?'

Arabella and another girl stood up at the same moment.

'Sit down, Arabella. We'll hear you next,' said Rita. 'What is it, Pamela?'

'It's a very silly complaint,' began Pamela, 'but it's an awful nuisance. You see, my cubicle is by the big window in my dormitory, and my monitor says it must be kept open when we are not there – and it must, of course – but on windy days all the things on my dressing-table blow out of the window and I'm always getting into trouble because they are found outside!'

Everyone laughed. Rita and William smiled. Joan, who was in Pamela's form, spoke to Rita. She was Pamela's monitor.

'Pamela is quite right,' she said. 'Anyone who has that cubicle has the same trouble. But we could move the dressing-table out of the window, if Matron wouldn't mind.'

'Ask her tomorrow,' said Rita. Matron was the one who saw to things of that sort, and she would see that the table was moved.

'Now, Arabella,' said William, noticing the angry, flushed face of the little girl, waiting her turn. Arabella stood up gracefully, not forgetting her little airs even in her rage.

'Please, William,' she said, in her smooth polite voice, a little shaken now by nervousness and anger, 'please, I have a very serious complaint to make.'

Everyone sat up straight. This was interesting and exciting. Serious complaints were worth listening to. All the first form looked at one another and pulled faces. Was Arabella going to complain about them? Well – she was very silly then, because her own secret would be bound to come out!

'What is your complaint?' asked William.

'Well,' said Arabella, 'ever since I have been to this school the children in my class – all except Rosemary – have been absolutely horrid to me. I can't tell you the things they do to me!'

'I think you must tell me,' said William. 'It's no use making a complaint and not saying what it really is. I can't believe that the whole form have been horrid to you.'

'Well, they have,' said Arabella, almost in tears. 'Julian is the worst. He – he holds his nose whenever he comes near me!'

There were a few giggles at this. Julian laughed loudly too. Arabella glared at him. Elizabeth, up on the monitor's platform, looked most surprised. She was the only one who did not know the real reason for the first form's treatment of Arabella, and she thought it was very foolish of the girl to complain of ordinary teasing. She had not known there was a real reason behind it all. But now she guessed that there was.

Arabella went on with her complaints. 'Then there is Jenny. She mimics me and mocks me whenever she can. I'm a new girl and it's very unkind. I haven't done anything to make them so unkind to me. It makes me very unhappy. I shall write to my mother. I shall . . .'

'Be quiet,' said Rita, seeing that Arabella was working herself up in a real tantrum. 'Be quiet now, and sit down. We will go into this. You shall have another chance to speak later, if you want to. But wait a minute – have you told your monitor about this?'

'No,' said Arabella sulkily. 'She doesn't like me either.'

Elizabeth went red. That was true. She had *shown* that she didn't like Arabella too – and so Arabella hadn't come to her for help or advice before putting everything before the Meeting. Oh, dear – that was a pity!

'Oh,' said Rita, glancing at Elizabeth. 'Well, now, let me see. We'll hear Jenny first. Jenny, will you please explain your unkind behaviour, and tell us if you have any real reason for it?'

Jenny stood up. Well – Arabella had brought all this on herself! She began to tell what she knew.

CHAPTER SEVEN

The Meeting deals with Arabella

'YOU SEE,' said Jenny, 'Arabella really brought all the trouble on herself. She didn't keep the rules, and we knew it, and so we didn't like her, and we teased her. That's all.'

'Oh, you storyteller!' said Arabella. 'I *have* kept the rules!'

'Arabella, be quiet,' said William. 'Who is Arabella's monitor? Oh – you are, Elizabeth Allen. Will you tell us, Elizabeth, if, in your opinion, Arabella has kept the rules?'

'Elizabeth doesn't know what we know,' said Jenny, interrupting. 'We know the deceitful and dishonest thing that Arabella did – but Elizabeth doesn't.'

Elizabeth looked very upset. How was it she hadn't known? She spoke to William.

'I'm afraid I don't know what Jenny is talking about, William,' she said. 'I know I ought to – because I'm a monitor and I should see all that goes on in the form – but I really don't know this.'

'Thank you,' said William gravely. He turned to Jenny. 'What have you to complain of about Arabella, Jenny?' he asked, with a glance at the fiery-red face of Arabella. The girl was full of horror now – whatever was Jenny going to say? She, Arabella, had meant to make a complaint, but she had never guessed that anyone else would complain about *her*.

Then, of course, it all came out.

'Arabella didn't put all her money into the Box last week. We know, because she bought a three pound book in the town and a lot of expensive chocolates,' said Jenny. 'She hid some in her music-case so that we wouldn't know. She told lies about it too. So, you see, William, we don't like her and we showed it. We thought perhaps she would be ashamed of herself if we teased her, and be honest next time and put all her money in.'

'I see,' said William. 'Sit down, Jenny.'

Everyone was now looking at Arabella. She didn't know what to say. How she wished she had never made her complaint! Whatever was she to do! This was simply dreadful.

'Arabella,' said Rita, 'what have you to say to this? Is it true?'

Arabella sat quite still and said nothing. Then a tear trickled down her cheek. She felt very, very sorry for herself. Why had her mother sent her to this horrid school where they had Meetings like this every week, and where no fault could be kept hidden?

'Arabella,' said Rita, 'please stand up. Is this true?'

Arabella's knees were shaking, but she stood up. 'Yes,' she said in a low voice. 'Some of it is true. But not all. You see – I didn't quite understand about putting *all* my money in. I did put in most of it. I wanted to ask my monitor, Elizabeth, about lots of things, but she seems to dislike me too, and – and . . .'

Elizabeth felt angry. Arabella was trying to put some of the blame on to *her*. She scowled at the girl and disliked her all the more.

'That's nonsense,' said Rita briskly. 'Elizabeth would always tell you anything, even if she did dislike you. Now listen, Arabella – you have behaved very foolishly, and you have only yourself to blame for the others' treatment of you. You will have to put things right.'

The head-girl turned to William and spoke in a low voice for a moment or two. He nodded. Rita spoke again. The whole school listened with interest.

'It is sometimes difficult for new children to understand and fall in with our rules,' said Rita in her clear voice. 'But after they have been here for a while, every boy and girl agrees that our rules are good. After all, we make them ourselves *for* ourselves, so it would be silly of us to make bad rules. We haven't very many, anyway. But what we have must be kept.'

'I see that,' said Arabella, who was still standing up. 'I'm sorry I broke that rule, Rita. If the others had told me I had broken the rule, and just scolded me and given me a chance to put *all* my money in next time, I'd have done it. But they didn't. They were just horrid and I didn't know why.'

'You will go to your monitor after this Meeting and give her all the money you have got, every penny. She will

put it into the Box. You will be allowed only fifty pence this week, for stamps, as you had so much extra last week.'

Arabella sat down, her cheeks flaming red again. Give her money to Elizabeth! Oh, dear, how she would hate that.

Rita had not quite finished with the matter. She spoke to the first form rather sternly.

'There is no need for you to take things in hand yourselves and do any punishing,' she said. 'After all, your monitors are there to give advice, and we have the Meeting each week to put anything right. You first-formers are not sensible enough to know how to treat a thing of this sort. You should have gone to Elizabeth.'

The first-formers looked uncomfortable and felt small.

'It is all rather a mountain made out of a molehill,' said William. 'Arabella is a new girl and didn't understand the importance of our rules. Now that she does she will keep them.'

A little more business was done at the Meeting and then the children filed out. Elizabeth went to Jenny.

'Why didn't you tell me about Arabella. It was mean of you not to. I did feel an idiot, sitting up there on the monitors' platform, hearing all this and not knowing a thing about it!'

'Yes – we ought to have told you,' said Jenny. 'I'm sorry. But, you see, we knew Arabella had been staying with you, and we thought it might be rather awkward, if she was a friend of yours.'

'Well, she's not,' said Elizabeth in a fierce tone, 'I can't bear her. She quite spoilt the last two weeks of my holidays for me.'

'Sh-sh, you idiot!' said Kathleen, giving her a nudge. Arabella was coming by, and must have overheard what was said.

'Arabella! You'd better get your money now and give it to me,' said Elizabeth hastily, hoping that Arabella hadn't overheard what she had just said. 'I'd like it now, whilst the School Box is out.'

Arabella was rather white. She said nothing, but went to her dormitory. She took out all the money she had hidden in various places.

She went downstairs again and found Elizabeth. Elizabeth, feeling rather awkward, held out her hand. Arabella crashed all the money into her palm, making Elizabeth cry out in pain. Some of the money went on the floor.

'There you are, you horrid thing!' said Arabella, her voice full of anger and tears. 'I suppose you were pleased to see me made fun of at the Meeting! Well, you didn't come out of it so well yourself, did you – the only person who didn't know anything! I'm sorry I spoilt your holidays – you may as well know that you spoilt mine too! I hated your home and everything in it, you most of all!'

Elizabeth was shocked and angry. She stared at Arabella, and spoke sharply.

'Pick up the money you've dropped. Pull yourself together, and don't talk to your monitor like that. Even if we don't like one another, we can at least be civil.'

'I can't imagine why anyone made *you* a monitor!' said Arabella in a scornful voice. 'Ill-mannered tomboy! I hate you!'

Arabella went quickly to the door, went through it, and slammed it after her. Elizabeth was left alone to pick up the money and put it into the Box. She was astonished at Arabella's fierceness, and worried too.

'Oh, dear, it's going to be very difficult to be a monitor in the first form if this sort of thing is going to happen,' thought Elizabeth, rattling the money into the Box.

As she went down the passage Arabella met Rita. The

head-girl saw her tear-stained face and stopped her kindly.

'Arabella, we all make mistakes at first so don't take things too much to heart. And do go to your monitor for advice and help,' said Rita. 'Elizabeth is a very wise little person, and very fair and just. I am sure she can always help you.'

This was not at all what Arabella wanted to hear at that moment. She was glad to have Rita's kind word but she did not want to hear praise of Elizabeth. As for going to Elizabeth for advice – well, she would never, *never* do that!

Rita went on her way, rather worried about Arabella, for she did not really feel that she was sorry for her mistake. If a person was really sorry, it was all right – they did try to do better. But if they were not sorry, only angry at being found out, then things went from bad to worse.

Elizabeth went to find Julian. 'I say, *you* might have warned me about Arabella,' she said. 'You really might. Why didn't you?'

'Couldn't be bothered,' said Julian. 'I don't care whether she puts her money into the Box or not – and I certainly don't care if she's teased or not. I like to do as I like – and I'm not interfering with other people. Let them do as *they* like.'

'But Julian,' said Elizabeth earnestly, 'you must see that we *can't* all do as we like, when so many of us live together. We—'

'Now don't start that goody-goody monitor talk,' said Julian at once. 'That's the only thing I don't like about you, Elizabeth – that you're a monitor. You seem to think it gives you a right to lecture me and make me into a Good Boy, and put everything right the way *you* think it should be.'

Elizabeth stared at Julian in dismay. 'Julian! How horrid of you! I'm very *proud* of being a monitor. It's mean of you to say it's the one thing you don't like about me. It's the thing I'm proudest of.'

'I wish I'd known you when you were the Naughtiest Girl in the School,' said Julian. 'I'd have liked you better then, I'm sure.'

'You wouldn't,' said Elizabeth crossly. 'I was silly then. Anyway, I'm just the same girl now as I was then, only I'm more sensible, and a monitor.'

'There you go again!' said Julian, heaving an enormous sigh. 'You simply can't forget for one moment that you are one of those grand, marvellous, and altogether wonderful beings – a *monitor*!'

He stalked away and left Elizabeth looking after him angrily. How stupid it was to have a friend who didn't like the thing you were proudest of! Really, Julian was most annoying at times!

CHAPTER EIGHT

Elizabeth lays a trap

SCHOOL LIFE went on its jolly way in that Easter term. Games were played and matches were won and lost. Many of the children who liked riding rode out every morning before breakfast. Robert always rode with Elizabeth, and the little girl chattered away to him as they rode.

'Do you like being a monitor, Elizabeth?' asked Robert one morning not long after the second Meeting of the school.

'Well,' said Elizabeth, and stopped to think. 'It's funny, Robert, I felt terribly proud when I was made a monitor – and I do still – but somehow it's set me a bit apart from the others, and I don't like that. And Julian will keep saying I'm goody-goody, and you know I'm not!'

'No, that's the very last thing you are,' said Robert with a grin. 'Well, I've never been a monitor or leader of any sort, Elizabeth, but I've often heard my uncle say that being set over others isn't altogether a happy thing at first – till you're used to it, and shake down into your new position.'

'I didn't like not being told about that Arabella business,' said Elizabeth. 'I felt left out. Last term I'd have been in the middle of it and heard everything. I think someone might have told me.'

'Well, we will, next time, I expect,' said Robert.

Elizabeth worked in the School Garden as hard as ever with John Terry. The crocuses they had planted together came up by the hundred, and looked wonderful in the early spring. The yellow ones came out first, and opened out well in the sunshine. Then the purple ones and the white ones came out together.

Julian's barrow was a great success. It was strange-looking, but strong and well made. The smaller boys loved using it.

'Thanks, Julian,' said John, 'that has saved us quite a large amount of money. I shall come to you when I want anything else!'

There was a great deal to do in the garden that term. There always was in the spring term. There was a good deal of digging to finish, and many things to plant. The children, under John's direction, sowed rows and rows of broad beans.

'Oh, dear, *must* we sow so many thousands, John?' groaned small Peter, standing up to straighten his back.

'Well, the whole school likes broad beans,' said John. 'It's nice to grow what people like.'

The children could keep pets if they liked, although they were not allowed to have cats or dogs, because these could not be kept in cages. Any child who had a pet had to look after it, and look after it well. If he or she did not, the pet was taken away from them – but that rarely happened, because the children were fond of their guinea-pigs, mice, budgies, pigeons, and so on, and took a great pride in keeping them clean and happy.

Arabella did not give Elizabeth any trouble in the next week or two, but she did not speak to her or have any more to do with her than she could help. She and Rosemary went about together, sometimes with Martin Follett. Julian made friends with everyone – or rather, every-one made friends with him, for he did not seem to care whether people were nice to him or not – but the boys and girls thought him an exciting and very clever person.

His only real friend was Elizabeth, and the two laughed and joked together a great deal. He did not say any more about her being a goody-goody monitor, and slowly Elizabeth began to get used to the idea that she was set over the others. In fact she sometimes forgot it altogether.

She was reminded of it when Rosemary came to her in trouble. 'Elizabeth – can I speak to you about something?' said the girl timidly.

'Of course,' said Elizabeth, remembering at once that she was a monitor, and must help, and act wisely.

'Well – I keep missing money,' said Rosemary, looking upset.

'*Missing* money!' said Elizabeth. 'What do you mean? Losing it, do you mean?'

'Well, I did think I was losing it at first,' said Rosemary.

'I thought I must have a hole in my pocket – but I haven't. I missed fifty pence last week. And yesterday a whole pound went – and you know what a lot that is out of two pounds, Elizabeth. And today twenty pence has gone out of my desk.'

Elizabeth was very astonished. She stared at Rosemary, and could hardly believe her ears.

'But Rosemary,' she said at last, 'Rosemary, you don't think anybody *took* your money!'

'Well, I do,' said Rosemary. 'I hate to say anything, Elizabeth, really I do. But I haven't any money left now except thirty pence, and that has to last me till the next Meeting, and I really must buy some stamps.'

'This is awful,' said Elizabeth. 'It's – it's stealing, Rosemary. Are you quite, quite sure of what you say?'

'Yes,' said Rosemary. 'Shall I make a complaint at the next Meeting?'

'No,' said Elizabeth grandly. 'I may be able to settle it myself. Then we can bring it before the Meeting, and we can tell them we settled the matter between us.'

'All right,' said Rosemary, who had no wish to get up and say anything before the Meeting. She was far too timid and weak! 'How will you settle it?'

'We'll lay a trap,' said Elizabeth. 'I'll think about it, Rosemary, and tell you. Don't tell anyone else.'

'Well – I did tell Martin Follett,' said Rosemary. 'I couldn't very well help it, because I was looking all over the place for my pound yesterday, and feeling very miserable at losing it – and he came in and was awfully kind. He helped me hunt for ages, and he offered me fifty pence of his own. So then I told him that I couldn't understand what was happening to my money. But I haven't told anyone else.'

'Well, don't,' said Elizabeth. 'We don't want to put anyone on their guard. I must say it was kind of Martin to offer you fifty pence, though.'

'He's very generous,' said Rosemary. 'He bought John Terry a packet of very special dwarf beans for the garden, you know. He said he wasn't keen on gardening himself, so that was his only way of doing his bit.'

'I wonder – I do wonder who could possibly be mean enough to take anyone's money,' thought Elizabeth as Rosemary went out of the room. 'What a horrible thing to do! Now, this really is a problem for me, and I must think about it. I'm a monitor, and I must try to put it right.'

She sat down and thought hard. She must find out the thief. Then she could deal with her – or him – and prove to everyone what a fine, sensible monitor she was. But how could she catch him?

'I know what I'll do,' said Elizabeth to herself. 'I'll show everyone the fine new pound I got out of the School Box last week, and then I'll put it in my desk – but I'll mark it first, so that I shall be able to know it again – and then watch to see if it disappears.'

So, the next day, when the children were playing in the

gym at break, because it was raining out-of-doors, Elizabeth took out her brand-new pound and showed it round.

'Look,' she said. 'It must have come out of the mint only last week, I should think! Isn't it bright and new?'

Ruth had a new pound as bright as gold, and she brought that out of her purse too. Robert had a new fifty pence bit.

'I shan't keep my shiny pound in my pocket, in case I get a hole there,' said Elizabeth. 'I shall put it in my desk, just under the ink-hole. It will be safe there.'

Before she put it there she marked a little cross on it with black Indian ink. Then she placed it under the ink-hole, in front of everyone, just before Miss Ranger came to take the class.

She glanced at Rosemary. The girl nodded her head slightly to tell Elizabeth that she knew why she had shown off her pound and put it into a safe place in front of everyone.

'Now we'll just see,' thought Elizabeth glancing round the class and wondering for the hundredth time which boy or girl could possibly be mean enough to take it.

The children left the schoolroom after morning lessons were finished and went to have a quick run and play in the garden. Then they had to come in to wash before dinner.

Elizabeth ran into the classroom to see whether her pound was still in its place. She opened her desk. Yes –

her pound was still there. She felt glad. Perhaps Rosemary was mistaken after all!

It was still there when afternoon school began. Rosemary looked across at her and Elizabeth nodded her head to tell her that the money was still there. Suppose the thief did not take it? Elizabeth would have to think of something else.

The pound was still there after tea. Rosemary came up to Elizabeth. 'Don't leave your pound there any more,' she said. 'I don't want it to be taken. You might not get it back – and a whole pound lost would be dreadful.'

'I'll leave it there till tomorrow,' said Elizabeth. 'Just to see.'

In the morning, before school, the little girl slipped along to the classroom. She opened her desk and felt for the bright new pound.

It wasn't there. It was gone. Although she had half expected this, Elizabeth was really shocked. So there *was* a thief in the class – a mean, horrible thief. Who was it? Well – wait till she saw that marked pound – then she would know!

CHAPTER NINE

Elizabeth gets a shock

IT WAS one thing to mark a coin so that she would know it again when she saw it, but another thing to make a plan to find it in someone's keeping! Elizabeth wondered and wondered how she could manage this.

After tea that day it was still raining and the children gathered together in their common-room. It was a cheerful room with wide windows, a big fireplace, a gramophone and a wireless, and lockers for all the children to keep their things in. It was the room the children liked best and felt to be really their own.

There was a merry noise that evening. The wireless was going, and the gramophone too, so that the one or two who wanted to read groaned aloud, and went to turn off either the wireless or the gramophone.

But as these were immediately turned on again by somebody else, it was a waste of time to turn them off!

'I say! Let's play a game of some sort,' said somebody. 'I've got a good race-game here. Let's all play it. There are twelve horses to race.'

'Right,' said the children, and watched Ruth put out the big game. It almost covered the table. There was a little squabbling over which horses to choose, and then the game began.

It was fun to be playing a game all together like this, and it was exciting to move the horses along the big board.

'Blow!' said Harry. 'I've landed in the middle of a ditch. I've got to go back six. One – two – three – four – five – six!'

The game was played to the end. Belinda won, and was presented with a bar of chocolate. Then Kathleen got out a game of her own. It was a spinning game. There were many little tops, all of different colours to be spun. They spun beautifully, making a tiny whirring sound as they did so.

Seeing the tops spinning gave Elizabeth an idea. She banged on the table.

'Let's all see if we can spin coins. Who is the best at it?'

The children put their hands into their pockets and brought out money. Some had pennies, some ten pences, some fifty pences, and one or two of them had pounds.

Julian had been far and away the best at spinning the tops. He could make them jump and hop across the table in a marvellous way. Now he showed how clever he was with coins.

'See my penny hop!' he cried, and spun it deftly on the polished table-top. It hopped and skipped as it spun in a marvellous way. Nobody else could do the trick.

'Watch me spin a pound on the top of a glass!' said

Julian. 'It will make a peculiar noise. Fetch a glass, somebody.'

A glass appeared and was put on the table. Everyone watched Julian. His green eyes gleamed with pleasure as he saw the admiring looks around him. He spun the coin on the bottom of the upturned glass, and it made a very funny noise.

'Like singing a little song,' said Ruth. 'Let *me* try, Julian.'

The pound fell off the glass, and Ruth picked it up. She tried her best to spin it, but it hopped off the glass at once and rolled off the table beside Elizabeth. The little girl bent to pick it up.

It was a bright new one. Elizabeth glanced at it, thinking it was funny that there should be a second brand-new pound coin in the form – and then she saw something that gave her a terrible shock.

She saw the tiny black cross she had made on the coin! She stared at it in the greatest dismay. It was her own pound, her very own, the one she had shown every-one, the one she had marked and put into her desk.

'Come on, Elizabeth – hand over the pound!' said Ruth impatiently. 'Anyone would think you had never seen a pound before, the way you are staring at it!'

Elizabeth threw the coin across to Ruth. Her hand was trembling. Julian! *Julian* had her pound. But Julian was her friend. He couldn't have her pound. But he had – he had! He had taken it out of his pocket. Elizabeth herself had seen him. The little girl stared miserably across at

Julian, who was watching Ruth with his deep-set eyes, a lock of black hair over his forehead as usual.

Rosemary had noticed Elizabeth's face. She had seen her staring at the pound. She knew that it must be the same one that the little girl had marked. She too looked in amazement at Julian.

Elizabeth was not going to say anything to Julian just then, but she could hardly wait for a chance to speak to him alone. She waited about that evening, hoping that she would find a chance. She thought and thought about the whole affair.

'Of course, I know Julian does just as he likes, and says so,' thought Elizabeth. 'He just doesn't care about anything or anybody. But after all, I am his friend, and he should care about what he does to *me*. He could have had my pound if he had asked me. How *could* he do such a thing?'

Then another thought came into her mind. 'I mustn't judge him till I hear what he says. Somebody may have lent it to him – or he may have given someone change for a pound. I must be careful what I say. I really must.'

Just before bed-time her chance came to speak to Julian alone. He went to get a book from the library, and Elizabeth met him in the passage as he came back.

'Julian,' she said, 'where did you get your nice bright pound from?'

'From the School Box last week,' said Julian, at once. 'Why?'

'Are you sure?' said Elizabeth. 'Oh, Julian, are you quite, quite sure?'

'Of course I am, idiot. Where else can we get money from?' said Julian, puzzled. 'What are you looking so upset about? What's the matter with my pound?'

Elizabeth was about to say that it was *her* pound, when she stopped. No – she mustn't say that, or Julian would know she was accusing him of taking it from her. He was her friend. She couldn't accuse him of anything so dreadful. She must think about it.

'Nothing's the matter with the pound,' she answered at last, thinking that something must be dreadfully the matter with Julian.

'All right then, don't look so peculiar,' said Julian, getting impatient. 'It's *my* pound – out of the School Box – and that's that.'

He stalked off, looking puzzled and annoyed. Elizabeth stared after him. Her mind was in a complete muddle. Of all the people in the form, the one she had never even thought of for one moment as the thief was Julian.

She slipped into a music-room by herself and began to play a sad and gloomy piece on the piano. Richard, who was passing, looked in in surprise.

'Gracious, Elizabeth! Why are you playing like that? Anyone would think you had lost a pound and found a penny!'

This old saying was half true at the moment, and Elizabeth gave a choky laugh. 'Well – I *have* lost a pound

– but I haven't found a penny,' she said.

'Golly, Elizabeth, you're not making yourself miserable over a pound, are you?' said Richard. 'I've never heard you playing so dolefully before. Cheer up.'

'Richard, listen – I'm not silly enough to be miserable over a pound,' said Elizabeth. 'It's something else.'

'Well, tell me then,' said Richard. 'I shan't tell anyone else, you know that.'

This was true. Elizabeth looked at Richard, and thought perhaps he could help her.

'Suppose you had a friend, and suppose he did something simply terribly mean to you – what would you do?' she asked.

Richard laughed. 'If it really was my friend – well, I wouldn't believe it!' he said. 'I'd know there was some mistake.'

'Oh, Richard, I think you're right,' said Elizabeth. 'I just won't believe it!'

She began to play the piano again, a happier tune. Richard grinned and left Elizabeth. He was used to her troubles by now. She was always getting into some difficulty or bother!

'Richard is right,' thought Elizabeth. 'I shan't believe it. It's some accident that Julian has got that pound. I'll have to begin all over again and find some way to catch the real thief.'

So she was just as friendly to Julian as ever, though Rosemary, who knew what had happened, was very puzzled to see it. She spoke to Elizabeth about it.

'It couldn't have been Julian,' said Elizabeth shortly. 'It must have been someone else. He got that pound out of the School Box. He said he did, when I asked him. There is some mistake.'

The next day Rosemary came to Elizabeth again. 'Listen,' she said, 'what do you think has happened? *Arabella* has lost some money now! Do you suppose it's the thief at work again?'

'Oh, golly!' said Elizabeth. 'I was so hoping that nothing more would happen. How much has Arabella lost?'

'Fifty pence,' said Rosemary. 'She put it into her mac pocket, and left it there – and when she went to get it, it was gone. And, Elizabeth, Belinda left some chocolate in her desk – and that's gone too. Isn't it awful?'

'Yes – it is,' said Elizabeth. 'How hateful it all is! Well – I'm absolutely determined to find out who the thief is now – and I'll haul him or her in front of the Meeting at once!'

The next thing that disappeared was sweets out of Elizabeth's locker. She went to get them – and they were not there!

'Blow!' said Elizabeth, angry and shocked. 'This is getting worse. I wish I knew who had my sweets.'

She soon knew. In class that afternoon Julian screwed up his face as if he wanted to sneeze. He pulled a hanky out of his pocket quickly, and something fell out. It was a sweet.

'One of *my* sweets!' said Elizabeth angrily to herself. 'The beast! He's taken my sweets. Then he must have taken that pound too. And he calls himself my friend!'

CHAPTER TEN

A dreadful quarrel

THE MORE Elizabeth thought about the stolen money and sweets, the angrier she felt with Julian. It *must* be Julian – but how could he do such a thing?

'He's always saying he does as he likes, so I suppose he takes other people's things if he wants them,' thought the little girl. 'He's bad. I know he's clever and amusing and jolly – but he's bad. I shall have to speak to him.'

She could hardly wait till the afternoon class was over. She paid no attention whatever to her lessons and Miss Ranger glanced at her sharply two or three times. Elizabeth did not seem to hear any questions at all, but simply gazed into space, with an angry look in her eyes.

'Elizabeth, I suppose you know you are in class?' said Miss Ranger at last. 'You have not answered a single question for the last half-hour.'

'I'm sorry, Miss Ranger,' said Elizabeth hastily. 'I – I was thinking of something else.'

'Well, will you kindly think of what you are supposed to be doing?' said Miss Ranger.

So Elizabeth had to try and forget Julian's misdeeds for a while, and think of Mary, Queen of Scots. But somehow her thoughts always slid away to Julian.

She looked at the boy, who sat in front of her. He was writing, his lock of black hair falling over his face. He brushed it impatiently away from time to time. Elizabeth wondered why he didn't have his hair cut shorter. Then it wouldn't worry him so. He looked round and grinned at her, his green eyes rather like a goblin's.

Elizabeth would not smile back. She bent her head down to her book, and Julian looked surprised. Elizabeth was usually ready with her smiles.

The class went rushing off at four o'clock – all except Elizabeth, who had to stay in and copy out some work for Miss Ranger. She was annoyed at this but not really surprised, for she knew she had not done any work at all that afternoon. So she raced through it, her mind still thinking of what she should say to Julian. She must get him alone somewhere.

It was tea-time when she had finished. She went to have her tea, but because she was upset she could not eat much, and the others teased her.

'She's sickening for measles or something,' said Harry. 'I've never seen Elizabeth off her food before. There must be something wrong with her!'

'Don't be funny,' said Elizabeth crossly.

Harry looked surprised.

'What's the matter? Are you all right?'

Elizabeth nodded. Yes – *she* was all right, but something else was all wrong. Oh, dear. She didn't want to tackle Julian, and yet she wouldn't have any peace of mind till she did.

She went to Julian after tea. 'Julian, I want to talk to you. It's very important.'

'Can't it wait?' asked Julian. 'I want to finish a job I'm doing.'

'No. It can't wait,' said Elizabeth. 'It's really, really important.'

'All right,' said Julian. 'I'll come and hear this terribly important thing.'

'Come into the garden,' said Elizabeth. 'I want to talk to you where we can't be overheard.'

'Well – I'll come to the stables,' said Julian. 'There won't be anybody about there now. You're very mysterious, Elizabeth.'

They walked together to the stables. No one was to be seen there at all. 'Now, what is it?' said Julian. 'Hurry up, because I want to get on with my job. I'm mending a spade for John.'

'Julian. Why did you take that money – and the chocolate and my sweets?' asked Elizabeth.

'What money – and what sweets?' said Julian.

'Oh, don't pretend you don't know!' cried Elizabeth losing her temper. 'You took my pound – and you must have taken Rosemary's money too – and I *saw* one of my sweets drop out of your pocket this afternoon when you pulled out your hanky to sneeze.'

'Elizabeth, how *dare* you say these things to me?' said

Julian, his face going red, and his green eyes getting very deep in colour.

'I dare because I'm a monitor, and I know all about your meanness!' said Elizabeth in a low, angry voice. 'You called yourself my friend – and . . .'

'Well, I like that! *You* call yourself *my* friend – and yet you say these hateful things to me!' said Julian in a loud voice, also losing his temper. 'Just because you're a monitor you think you have the right to go round accusing innocent people of horrible tricks. You're not fit to be anyone's friend. You aren't mine any longer.'

He began to walk off, but Elizabeth ran after him, her eyes blazing. She caught hold of his coat-sleeve. Julian tried to shake her off.

'You've got to listen to me, Julian!' almost shouted Elizabeth. 'You've got to! Do you want all this to be brought out at the next Meeting?'

'If you dare to say anything to anyone else, I'll pay you out in a way you won't like,' said Julian, between his teeth. 'All girls are the same – catty and dishonourable – making wild statements that aren't true – and not even believing people when they do tell the truth!'

'Julian! I don't want to bring it up at the Meeting,' cried Elizabeth. 'I don't – I don't. That's why I'm giving you this chance of telling me, so that I can help you and put things right. You always say you do as you like – so I suppose you thought you could take anything you wanted – and . . .'

'Elizabeth, I *do* do as I like – but there are many many things I don't like, and would never do,' said Julian, his green eyes flashing, and his black brows coming down low over them. 'I don't like stealing – I don't like lying – I don't like tale-telling. So I don't do those things. Now I'm going. You're my worst enemy now, not my best friend. I shall never, never like you again.'

'I'm not your worst enemy, I want to help you,' said Elizabeth. 'I saw my own marked pound, I tell you. I saw my own sweet come out of your pocket. I'm a monitor, so I . . .'

'So you thought you had the right to accuse me, and you thought I'd confess to something I don't happen to have done, and you thought I'd cry on your shoulder and promise my monitor to be a good little boy,' said Julian in a horrid voice. 'Well, you are mistaken, my dear Elizabeth. Why anyone made you a monitor I can't think!'

He walked away. Elizabeth by now was in a real temper, and she tried to pull him back once more. Julian turned in a rage, took hold of Elizabeth by the shoulders and shook her so hard that her teeth rattled in her head.

'If you were a boy I'd show you what I really think of you!' said Julian in a low, fierce voice. He suddenly let Elizabeth go and walked off, his hands deep in his pockets, his hair untidy, and his mouth in a straight, angry line.

Elizabeth felt rather weak. She leaned against the stable wall and tried to get back her breath. She tried to think clearly, but she couldn't. What a dreadful, dreadful thing to happen!

Footsteps nearby made her jump. Martin Follett came out of the stable, looking very white and scared.

'Elizabeth! I couldn't help hearing. I didn't like to come out and interrupt. Elizabeth, I'm so sorry for you. Julian had no right to be so beastly when you were trying your hardest to help him.'

Elizabeth felt grateful for Martin's friendly words, but she was sorry he had overheard everything.

'Martin, you're not to say a word to anyone about this,' she said, standing up straight again, and pushing back her curls. 'It's very private and secret. Do you promise?'

'Of course,' said Martin, 'but, Elizabeth, let me help a bit. I'll give you some of my sweets. And I'll give you a pound to make up for the one you lost. That will put things right, won't it? Then you needn't bother Julian any more, or quarrel with him. You needn't bring the matter up at the Meeting either.'

'Oh, Martin, it's all very kind of you,' said Elizabeth, feeling very tired suddenly, 'but you don't see the point. It's not my pound or my sweets I mind, silly – it's the fact that Julian has been taking them. You can't put *that* right, can you! Giving me a pound and your sweets won't help Julian to stop taking what isn't his. I should have thought you could have seen that.'

'Well – give him a chance,' said Martin earnestly. 'Don't report him at the Meeting. Just give him a chance.'

'I'll see,' said Elizabeth. 'I'll have to think it all out. Oh, dear, I wish I wasn't a monitor. I wish I could go to a monitor for help! I don't seem much use as a monitor myself. I can't even think what I ought to do.'

Martin slipped his arm through hers. 'Come and have a talk with John about the garden,' he said. 'That will do you good.'

'You're kind to me, Martin,' said Elizabeth gratefully. 'But I don't want to talk to John. I don't want to talk to anybody just now. I want to think by myself. So leave me, please, Martin. And, Martin, you do *promise* not to tell anyone about this, don't you? It's Julian's business and mine, not anybody else's.'

'Of course I promise,' said Martin, looking straight at Elizabeth. 'You can trust me, Elizabeth. I'll leave you now, but if I can help you any time, I will.'

He went, and Elizabeth thought how nice he was. 'I'm sure he won't tell anyone,' she thought. 'It would be so awful if the others got to know about this. I simply don't know what to do. Julian will really hate me now. If only things would blow over!'

But they didn't blow over. They got very much worse. Julian was not the kind of boy to forget and forgive easily, and he was certainly not going to make things easy for Elizabeth. She had been his best friend – now she was his worst enemy! Look out then, Elizabeth!

CHAPTER ELEVEN

Julian plays a trick

EVERYONE SOON noticed that Julian and Elizabeth were no longer friends. Elizabeth looked thoroughly miserable and upset, and Julian took no notice of her at all.

Arabella was pleased. She liked and admired Julian tremendously, for all his careless, untidy ways. She had been annoyed when he had chosen Elizabeth for his friend. She would have liked to have been chosen instead.

'He's got simply marvellous brains!' said Arabella to Rosemary, who, not having many herself, sincerely admired those who had. 'He could do anything, that boy! I think he will be a wonderful inventor when he grows up – really *do* something in the world!'

'Yes, I think so too,' said Rosemary, agreeing with Arabella, as she always did. 'Arabella, I wonder why Elizabeth and Julian have quarrelled. They haven't spoken a word to one another all day – and whenever Julian does take a look in Elizabeth's direction, it's really fierce!'

'Yes – I'd like to know too why they've quarrelled,' said Arabella, 'I think I'll ask Julian. Perhaps he would like to be friends with us, now that's he's quarrelled with Elizabeth.'

So Arabella asked Julian that afternoon. 'Julian, I'm sorry to see that you and Elizabeth have quarrelled,' she said in her sweetest voice. 'I'm sure it must have been Elizabeth's fault. Why did you quarrel?'

'Sorry, Arabella, but I'm afraid that's my own business,' said Julian rather shortly.

'You might tell me,' said Arabella. 'I am on your side, not Elizabeth's. I never did like Elizabeth.'

'There aren't any sides, as you call it,' said Julian.

And that was all that Arabella could get out of Julian. She felt cross about it and more curious than ever. Whatever could the matter be? It must be something serious or Elizabeth wouldn't look so worried.

'I do wish we could find out,' she said to Rosemary. 'I really do wish we could.'

'What do you want to find out?' asked Martin, coming up behind them.

'Why Elizabeth and Julian have quarrelled,' said Arabella. 'You haven't any idea, have you, Martin?'

'Well – I do know something,' said Martin. Arabella stared at him in excitement.

'Tell us,' she said.

'Well,' said Martin, 'it's a dead secret. You mustn't tell anyone at all. Promise?'

'Of course,' said Arabella, not meaning to keep the secret at all. 'Who told you, Martin?'

'Well – Elizabeth told me herself,' said Martin.

'Then you can quite well tell us,' said Arabella at once.

'If Elizabeth told *you*, she will be sure to tell the others too.'

So Martin told the secret – how Elizabeth had accused Julian of stealing money and sweets, and how he had denied it angrily. Arabella's big eyes nearly fell out of her head as she listened. Rosemary could hardly believe it either.

'Oh, how beastly of Elizabeth!' said Arabella. 'How could she, Martin? I'm sure that however don't-careish Julian is, he is honest!'

Soon the secret was out all over the form. Everyone knew why Julian and Elizabeth had quarrelled. Everyone spoke about stolen money and sweets, Julian and Elizabeth.

'I think Julian ought to know that Elizabeth has spread the tale about him,' said Arabella to Rosemary. 'I really do. It's not fair.'

'But did she spread it?' asked Rosemary doubtfully. 'It was Martin that told us.'

'Well, he said Elizabeth told *him*, didn't she – and if she told him, she would probably have told others,' said Arabella. 'After all, everyone knows now, so I expect Elizabeth did a lot of the telling.'

Rosemary felt a little uncomfortable. She knew how much Arabella herself had told, and she knew too that Arabella had added a little to the story. But Rosemary was too weak to argue with her friend. So she said nothing.

Arabella spoke to Julian the next day. 'Julian,' she

said, 'I do think it is mean of Elizabeth to spread that tale of you taking things – you know, money and sweets. I do really.'

Julian looked as if he could not believe his ears. 'What do you mean?' he asked at last.

'Well – it's all over the form now that you and Elizabeth quarrelled because she said you took things that belonged to other people, and you denied it,' said Arabella. She slipped her arm through Julian's. The boy had gone very pale.

'Don't worry, Julian,' she said. 'We all know what Elizabeth is! Goodness knows why she was made a monitor! Who would go to *her* for help, I'd like to know! She's not to be trusted at all.'

'You're right,' said Julian, 'but I thought she was. I never imagined for one moment she would spread such a story. A monitor, too! She's a little beast. I can't think why I ever liked her.'

'No, I'm sure you can't,' said Arabella, delighted. 'Fancy her going all round the form whispering these horrible things about you – and you haven't said a word about *her*!'

Of course, Elizabeth had not said a word either, but Julian did not know that. He had not known that Martin had overheard everything, and he thought that if the story got round, it could only have been told to the others by Elizabeth herself. He thought very bitterly of her indeed.

'I'll pay her back for that,' he said to Arabella.

'I should,' said Arabella eagerly. 'As I told you before, Julian, I'm on your side, and so is Rosemary. I expect lots of others are too.'

This time Julian did not say anything about there being no sides. He was hurt and angry, and the only thing he wanted to do was to get back at Elizabeth and hurt her.

And then many curious things began to happen to Elizabeth. Julian used all his clever brains to think out tricks that would get her into trouble – and when Julian really used his brains things began to happen!

Julian sat just in front of Elizabeth in class. In one lesson, history, the children had to have out a good many books, which they put in a neat pile on the back of their desks, so that they might refer quickly to them when they needed to.

Julian invented a curious little gadget like a spring. He twisted the spring up in a peculiar way so that it took a long time to untwist itself. He slipped it under Elizabeth's pile of books.

The lesson began. Miss Ranger was not in a good temper that day, for she had a headache, so the children were being rather careful not to make noises. Nobody let their desk-lids fall with a slam, nobody dropped anything.

Julian grinned to himself, as he worked quietly in front of Elizabeth. He knew that the peculiar little spring was slowly untwisting itself under the bottom book. It was extremely strong, and when it reached a certain twist it would spring wide open and force the books off the desk.

Sure enough, this happened after about five minutes had gone by. The spring gave itself a final twist and the books moved. The top one fell, and then the others, all in a pile to the floor.

Miss Ranger jumped. 'Whose books fell then?' she said crossly. 'Elizabeth, don't be careless. How did that happen?'

'I don't know, Miss Ranger,' said Elizabeth, puzzled. 'I really don't.'

Julian bent to pick up the books, which had fallen just behind. He put another, twisted spring under the bottom one again, pocketing the first one, which had fallen to the floor with the books.

In five minutes' time that spring worked too. It was a stronger one, and the books shot off the desk in a hurry. Crash, crash, crash, crash, crash!

Miss Ranger jumped violently, and her fountain-pen, which she was using, made a blot on the book she was correcting.

'Elizabeth! Are you doing this on purpose?' she cried. 'If it happens again you will go out of the room. I will not have you disturbing the class like this.'

Elizabeth was extremely puzzled. 'I'm very sorry, Miss Ranger,' she said. 'Honestly, the books seemed to jump off my desk by themselves.'

'Don't be childish, Elizabeth,' said Miss Ranger. 'That's the kind of thing a child in the lower school might say to me.'

Julian picked up the books, grinning. Elizabeth gave him a furious look. She had no idea that he was playing a trick on her, but she didn't like the grin. Once more Julian placed one of his curious springs under the bottom book.

And once again all the books jumped off the desk in a hurry. This time Miss Ranger lost her temper.

'Go out of the room,' she snapped at Elizabeth. 'Once might have been an accident – even twice – but not three times. I'm ashamed of you. You're a monitor and should know how to behave.'

With scarlet cheeks Elizabeth went out of the room. In her first term she had *tried* to be sent out of the room – but now she felt it to be a great disgrace. She hated it. She stood outside the door, almost ready to cry for shame and anger.

'It wasn't my fault. My books really *did* seem to jump off by themselves. I never even touched the beastly things!' she thought.

And then, how dreadful! Who should come by but Rita, the head-girl herself. She looked in the greatest surprise at Elizabeth, standing red-faced outside the door. 'Why are you here, Elizabeth?' she asked gravely.

CHAPTER TWELVE

Elizabeth in disgrace

'I WAS sent out of the room, Rita,' said Elizabeth, 'but it was for something that wasn't my fault. Please believe me.'

'Don't let it happen again, Elizabeth,' said Rita. 'You know that you are a monitor, and should set an example to the others. I am not very pleased with various things I have heard about you and the first form this term.'

She walked down the passage and Elizabeth stared after her, wondering what Rita knew She felt suddenly very sad and gloomy. 'I looked forward to this term so much,' she thought, 'and now everything is going wrong.'

She was called back into the room at the end of the lesson, and Miss Ranger spoke a few stern words to her. Elizabeth knew that it was no good saying again that she had not made the books fall, so she said nothing.

The next trick that Julian thought of was most extraordinary. He grinned with delight when it came into his mind. He went into the laboratory, where the children did most of their science work, and mixed up various chemicals together. He made them into a few wet little pellets and put them into a box. Then, before afternoon school, he slipped into the empty classroom, moved

Elizabeth's desk, and put a table in its place.

He stood a chair on top of the table and then climbed up and stood on it. He could reach the ceiling then. He arranged the little wet pellets close together on the white ceiling. He brushed them quickly over with a queer-smelling liquid. This would have the effect of making the little pellets gradually swell and burst, letting out a large drop of water which would fall straight downwards.

'This is a good trick,' thought Julian, as he jumped down from the chair, put it back in its place, and pulled the table away. He put Elizabeth's desk back, arranging it exactly under the pellets on the ceiling. They were white and hardly noticeable.

That afternoon Mam'zelle came to take French. Elizabeth and the others had learnt French verbs and some French poetry. Mam'zelle was to hear it. All the children gabbled it to themselves before the lesson, making sure they knew it. Mam'zelle was heard coming along the passage and Elizabeth sprang to hold open the door.

Mam'zelle was in a good temper. The children were glad. Miss Ranger didn't get cross unless there really was something to be cross about – but Mam'zelle often got cross about nothing. Still, this afternoon she looked very pleasant indeed.

'And now we will have a very nice afternoon,' she said, beaming round. 'You will all say your verbs without one single mistake, and you will say your poetry most beautifully. And I shall be very pleased with you.'

No one made any reply to this. It would be nice if nobody made any mistake, but that was too much to be hoped for! Someone always came to grief in the French class.

Julian chose that afternoon to use his brains in the proper way. He rattled off his verbs without a single mistake. He addressed Mam'zelle in excellent French, so that she beamed all over her face with pleasure.

'Ah, this Julian! Always he pretends he is so stupid, but he is very clever! Now we will see if he knows his poetry well! Speak it to me, Julian.'

Julian began reciting the French smoothly and well. But no sooner had he begun than there came an interruption. It was Elizabeth.

She had been sitting down, her head bent over her French book. And right on the top of her head had come a big drop of water! Elizabeth was most astonished. She gave a small cry and rubbed the top of her head. It was wet!

'What is the matter, Elizabeth?' asked Mam'zelle impatiently.

'A drop of water fell on my head,' said Elizabeth, puzzled. She looked up at the ceiling, but there did not seem anything to be seen there.

'You are silly, Elizabeth,' said Mam'zelle. 'You do not expect me to believe that.'

'But a drop of water *did* fall on my head,' said Elizabeth. 'I felt it.'

Jenny and Robert began to giggle. They thought Elizabeth was making it up in order to have a bit of fun. Mam'zelle rapped sharply on her desk.

'Silence!' she said. 'Julian, go on with your poetry. Begin again.'

Julian began again, knowing that another drop or two would fall on Elizabeth's head shortly. He wanted to laugh.

'Oh! Oh!' said Elizabeth suddenly from behind him! Two drops had fallen splash on to her hair. The little girl simply couldn't understand it. She rubbed her head.

'Elizabeth! Once more you interrupt!' said Mam'zelle angrily. 'Are you trying to spoil Julian's work? He is doing it so well. What is the matter now? Do not tell me again that it is raining on your head!'

'Well, Mam'zelle, it *is*,' said Elizabeth, and she rubbed her hand in her wet hair. Everyone roared with laughter. Mam'zelle began to get really angry.

'Silence, everybody!' she cried. 'I will not have this noise. Elizabeth, I am surprised at you. A monitor should not behave like this.'

'But Mam'zelle, honestly, it's very odd,' began Elizabeth again – and then another drop fell on her hair. She gave a jump and looked up at the ceiling. She really felt very puzzled indeed.

'Ah! You look at the ceiling as if it was the sky? You think it is raining on you! You think you will play me a silly joke!' cried Mam'zelle, her eyes beginning to flash. Everyone sat up, enjoying the fun. It was exciting when Mam'zelle lost her temper.

'Well, can I sit somewhere else?' asked Elizabeth in despair. 'Something does keep dropping on my head and I don't like it.'

'You can go and sit outside the room,' said Mam'zelle sternly. 'This is the silliest joke I have ever heard of. You will ask next if you can bring an umbrella into my class and sit with it over your head.'

The whole class squealed with laughter at the thought of this. But Mam'zelle had not meant to be funny, and she banged angrily on her desk.

'Silence! I do not make a joke. I am very angry. Elizabeth, leave my class.'

'Oh, please, Mam'zelle, no,' said poor Elizabeth. 'Please don't send me out of the room. I won't interrupt again. But, honestly, it's very strange.'

Another drop fell on her head, but she said nothing this time. She could not bear to be sent out of the room a second time, she really couldn't! She would rather get soaked through than that!

'Well – one more word from you and you will go,' threatened Mam'zelle. Elizabeth thankfully sat down, and made up her mind not even to jump if another of those unexpected drops landed on her hair.

But there was no more to come. Soon Elizabeth's hair was dry again, and nothing fell to wet it. She recited her verbs and poetry in her turn, and was allowed to remain in the room for the rest of the lesson.

Afterwards most of the children crowded round her. 'Elizabeth! How did you dare to act like that? Let's feel your head!'

But it was now dry, and no one would believe Elizabeth when she said over and over again that drops of water *had* fallen on her. They rubbed their hands over her hair, but not a bit of wetness was left.

'Why don't you own up to us and say it was a good joke?' asked Harry. 'You might just as well.'

'Because it *wasn't* a joke, it was real,' answered Elizabeth angrily.

The children went off. They all thought Elizabeth had played a joke, but they also thought it wasn't right not to own up to it afterwards.

'She's telling untruths,' said Arabella to Rosemary. 'Well, all I can say is – she's a funny sort of monitor to have!'

One or two of the others agreed. They had enjoyed the joke – but they really did think that Elizabeth had made up the story of the falling drops, and they felt rather disgusted with her when she denied it.

Mam'zelle related the story to Miss Ranger in the mistresses' common-room that day. 'It is not like Elizabeth to be so silly,' she said.

Miss Ranger looked puzzled. 'I don't understand her,' she said. 'She is not behaving like herself lately. She was very stupid in my class too – kept pushing piles of books over! So childish.'

'I thought she would make a good mon-itor,' said Mam'zelle. 'I am disappointed in Elizabeth.'

Arabella spoke against Elizabeth whenever she could, and some of the children listened. Arabella was clever in the way she spoke.

'Of course,' she said, 'I like a joke as much as anyone, and it's fun to play a trick in a dull lesson. But honestly I don't think a *monitor* should do that. I mean, I don't see why any of us shouldn't play the fool a bit if we like – but not a monitor. You do expect a monitor to behave – or why make them monitors?'

'She was called the Naughtiest Girl in the School two terms ago, wasn't she?' said Martin. 'Well, it must be difficult to stop being that, really. I think it was silly to make her a monitor. She couldn't have been ready to be one.'

'Look at the beastly stories she spread about poor Julian too,' said Arabella. 'A monitor should be the first to stop a thing like that, not start it. Well, I always did say I couldn't imagine why Elizabeth was a monitor.'

'Perhaps she won't be for long!' said Martin. 'I don't see why we should put up with someone who behaves like Elizabeth. How can we look up to her or go to her for advice? She oughtn't to *be* a monitor!'

Poor Elizabeth. She knew the children were whispering about her – and she couldn't do anything about it.

CHAPTER THIRTEEN

Arabella's secret

THE NEXT School Meeting came and went without anything being said by Elizabeth. The girl was so miserable and so puzzled as to what she should do for the best that she had made up her mind to say nothing, at least for the present.

Meanwhile Arabella was soon going to have a birthday. Her mother had promised to send her a big birthday cake, and whatever else she liked to ask for to eat or drink. Mrs Buckley was now in America, but Arabella could order what she liked from one of the big London stores.

Arabella talked about it a good deal. She loved to boast, and she talked of all the good things she would order.

Then she had an idea. She told it to Rosemary. 'What about a midnight feast, Rosemary? We had one once at my old school and it was such fun. We should have plenty to eat and drink – and think how exciting it would be to have it in the middle of the night!'

Rosemary agreed. 'Should we have it at midnight?' she asked. 'We couldn't very well have it earlier, because some of the mistresses and masters might be up.'

'Yes – we'll have it just after midnight,' said Arabella.

'But we won't ask Elizabeth! She's such a horrid thing she might give the secret away and spoil the feast!'

'All right,' said Rosemary. 'Well – who will you ask, then?'

'Everyone – except just a few who are Elizabeth's old friends,' said Arabella. 'We won't ask Kathleen – or Harry – or Robert. They still stick up for Elizabeth. Anyway, I suppose Elizabeth wouldn't come, even if we did ask her, because she might think a midnight feast was against the silly rules, and she's a monitor.'

So the first form once more had a secret that was whispered from one to the other. Elizabeth heard the talking, and noticed that it died down when she passed. She thought they must be whispering about her again, and she was angry and sad.

Julian was asked, of course, and Martin. Julian's green eyes gleamed when he heard of the midnight feast. This was just the sort of daring thing he liked.

The children discussed where they should hide the food and drink. They did not want the mistresses to guess what they were going to do.

'We'll show the birthday cake round, and have some of it for tea,' said Arabella, 'but we won't say anything about the other things.'

'Hide the ginger beers in one of the garden sheds,' said Martin. 'I know a good place. I'll put them there. I can fetch them on the night.'

'And put the biscuits in the old games locker in the

passage,' said Julian. 'It's never used, and no one will see it there. I'll take them along.

So the goodies were hidden here and there, and the children began to feel most excited. The few that were left out did not know what was happening. They only knew that it was Arabella's secret, and that a great fuss was being made of it.

Arabella always made a point of talking in a low voice about the party whenever she saw Elizabeth coming near. Then she would give a jump when she looked up and saw Elizabeth, nudge the person she was talking to and change the subject quickly and loudly.

This annoyed Elizabeth very much. 'You need not think I want to hear your stupid secret,' she said to Arabella. 'I don't. So talk all you like about it – I'll shut my ears!'

All the same, it was not pleasant to be left out. Neither was it pleasant to see Julian talking and laughing to Arabella and Rosemary. She did not know that he did it sometimes to annoy her. He could not bring himself to like the boastful, vain little Arabella very much. But if his friendship with her annoyed Elizabeth, then he would certainly go on with it!

Arabella's birthday came. The children wished her many happy returns of the day and gave her little presents, which she accepted graciously, with pretty words of thanks. There was no doubt that Arabella knew how to behave when she was getting her own way!

Elizabeth gave Arabella nothing – neither did she wish

her a happy birthday. She saw Julian give her a beautiful little brooch he had made with his own clever hands. Arabella pinned it on joyfully.

'Oh, Julian!' she said loudly, knowing that Elizabeth could hear. 'You *are* a good friend! Thank you ever so much.'

The midnight feast was to be held in the common-room. This room was well away from any of the mistresses' bedrooms, and the children felt they would be safe there. They all felt excited that day, and Miss Ranger wondered what could be the matter with her class.

Quite by chance Elizabeth opened the old games locker in the passage. She was hunting for a ball to practise catching with on the lacrosse field, and she thought there might possibly be one there. She stared in surprise at the bag of biscuits.

'I suppose Miss Ranger put them there,' she thought, 'Perhaps she has forgotten them. I must tell her. She may want them for the biscuits to give out at break.'

But Elizabeth forgot all about them and didn't say anything to Miss Ranger. She had no idea that they belonged to Arabella, and were going to be eaten at the feast.

Arabella's secret was well kept. The children who had been asked really were afraid that if Elizabeth got to know it she might try to stop it, as she was a monitor. So they carefully said nothing at all to her. She and a few others were quite in the dark about it.

When midnight came all the children but Arabella were asleep. She had said she would keep awake and tell everyone when it was time. She was so excited that she had no difficulty at all in keeping her eyes wide open until she heard the school clock strike midnight from its tower.

She sat up in bed and groped for her dressing-gown. She put on her slippers. Then, taking a small torch she went to wake her friends, giving them little nudges.

They awoke with jumps. 'Sh!' whispered Arabella to each one. 'Don't make a noise! It's time for the midnight feast.'

Elizabeth was sound asleep, and so was Kathleen. They did not wake when the others padded out of their room to meet the boys, who were now coming from their own part of the school to the common-room. There was a lot of whispering, and choked-back giggles could be heard all the way down the passages.

The children crowded into the common-room and lighted candles. They were afraid to put on the electric light in case the strong light showed through the blinds.

'Anyway, it's more fun to have candles!' said Arabella gleefully. This was the kind of thing she liked. She was queen of the party! She wore a beautiful silk dressing-gown and blue silk slippers to match. She really looked lovely, and she knew it.

The children set out the food and drink. What a lovely lot there was!

'Sardines! I love those!' said Ruth.

'Tinned peaches! Oooh! How lovely!'

'Bags I some of those chocolate buns! They look as if they would melt in my mouth!'

'Pass that spoon, someone. I'll ladle out the peaches.'

'Don't make such a noise, Belinda. That's twice you've dropped a fork! You'll have Miss Ranger here if you don't look out.'

Pop! A ginger-beer bottle was opened and another and another. Pop! Pop! The children looked at one another, delighted. This was really fun. It was past midnight – and here they were eating and drinking all kinds of lovely things!

'Where are the biscuits?' said Arabella. 'I feel as if I'd like a biscuit to eat with these peaches. I can't see the biscuits. Where are they?'

'Oh – I forgot to get them,' said Julian, getting up. 'I'll fetch them now, Arabella. I won't be a minute. They are in that games locker.'

He went out to fetch the biscuits, groping his way along the passage, then up the stairs to where the locker stood in a corner.

He had no torch and it was dark. He stumbled along, trying to be as quiet as possible. He walked into a chair, and knocked it over with a crash. He stood still, wondering if anyone had heard.

He was not far from the room where Elizabeth slept. When the chair went over, the little girl awoke with a jump. She sat up in bed, wondering what the noise was.

'I'd better go and see,' she thought. She slip-ped out of bed and put on her dressing-gown. She did not notice that half the beds were empty in the dormitory. She put on her slippers and crept to the door with her torch not yet switched on.

She went into the passage and stood there. She walked along a little way and thought she heard the noise of someone not very far in front of her. She padded softly down the passage.

The Someone went to the old games locker. Elizabeth distinctly heard the creak as it was opened. Who could it be? And what were they doing at that time of night?

Elizabeth walked softly up to the locker. She switched on her torch very suddenly, and made Julian almost jump out of his skin.

'Julian! What are you doing here? Oh – you rotten thief – you're stealing *biscuits* now! I think you're too disgusting for words! Put them back at once!'

'Sh!' hissed Julian. 'You'll wake everyone, you idiot.'

He did not attempt to put back the bag of biscuits. He meant to take them to the feast. But Elizabeth did not know that, of course. She honestly thought he had come there to steal the biscuits in the middle of the night.

'Well – I've really caught you this time!' she cried. 'Caught you with the stolen goods in your hand! You can't deny *that*! Give them to me!'

Julian snatched them away. The lid of the locker fell with a terrific bang that echoed all up and down the passage.

'Idiot!' said Julian, in despair. 'Now you've woken everyone!'

CHAPTER FOURTEEN

Sneezing powder

THE CRASH of the locker lid certainly had awakened a good many people. There came the sound of footsteps and of doors being opened. The mistresses would soon be on the scene.

Julian fled to warn the others, giving Elizabeth a furious push as he passed her. She almost fell over. She did not know where he had gone, so she ran back to her own dormitory, excited to think that she really had caught Julian in the very act of stealing the biscuits.

'Now I'll report him!' she thought, as she climbed into bed. 'I jolly well will!'

Julian ran to the common-room and opened the door. 'Quick!' he said. 'Get back to your beds. Elizabeth caught me as I was getting the biscuits, and made an awful noise. If you don't get back quickly, we'll all be caught.'

Hastily the children stuffed everything into their lockers round the wall, or into empty desks. Then they blew out the candles and fled, hoping that they had not left too many crumbs about.

The boys raced for their own dormitories. The girls rushed to theirs.

'Blow Elizabeth!' panted Arabella as she took off her

dressing-gown and slipped into bed. 'We were just in the middle of everything. Now it's all spoilt!'

The mistresses had been asking one another what the noise was. Mam'zelle, who slept nearest to the first-form dormitories, was a sound sleeper, and had heard nothing at all. She was surprised when Miss Ranger opened the door and woke her.

'Perhaps it is the girls in the first-form dormitories playing tricks on one another,' said Mam'zelle sleepily. 'You go and see, Miss Ranger.'

But, by the time that Miss Ranger went into the dormitories and switched on the lights, not a sound was to be heard. All the children seemed to be sleeping most peacefully. Too peacefully really, Miss Ranger thought!

Elizabeth saw the light switched on, and out of the corner of her eye she watched Miss Ranger. Should she tell her what had happened? No – she wouldn't. She would spring it on the School Meeting tomorrow, and make everyone sit up and take notice!

Miss Ranger switched off the light and went quietly back to bed. She couldn't imagine what the noise had been. Perhaps the school cat had been chasing about and upset something. Miss Ranger got into bed and fell asleep.

Elizabeth lay awake a long time, thinking of Julian and the biscuits. She was quite, quite sure now that Julian was a disgusting thief. All that talk about doing what he liked and letting others do what *they* liked! It was just a way of excusing himself for his bad ways.

'He'll get a shock when I stand up at the Meeting and report him,' thought Elizabeth.

The children were angry that Elizabeth should have brought their fun to such a sudden end. 'Shall we give her a good scolding?' said Arabella primly.

'Well – she doesn't know about the feast,' said Julian, 'though she must have wondered what you had all been up to when you crept back to bed so suddenly.'

Elizabeth *had* wondered – but she knew that Arabella had had a birthday and she had simply thought that the girls had visited her that night, and had a few games. She had not thought of a feast.

'Don't let's tell her,' said Julian. 'We could finish the feast tonight – and she might stop it if she guessed.'

So no one told Elizabeth that she had spoilt the feast, but they gave her many black looks which puzzled her very much.

Julian thought of a way to pay back Elizabeth for spoiling the fun of the night before. He told the others.

'Look,' he said, 'I've made some sneezing powder. I'll scatter some between the pages of Elizabeth's French book – and we'll all watch her get a sneezing fit in Mam'zelle's class.'

'Ooh yes!' said everyone in delight. This was a joke after their own hearts.

Julian slipped into the classroom before afternoon school. He went to Elizabeth's desk and opened it. He found her French book, and lightly scattered the curious sneezing powder over it. He had discovered it when he was inventing something else, and had found himself suddenly sneezing. Julian was always inventing something new, thinking of something that no one had thought of before!

He scattered the pages full of the white powder, then shut the book carefully and put it back. He slipped out of the classroom, grinning. Elizabeth would get a surprise in the French class. So would Mam'zelle.

The children went to their form-rooms when the bell rang for afternoon school. 'French!' groaned Jenny. 'Oh dear. I'm sure I shall forget everything if Mam'zelle is in a bad temper.'

'I feel so sleepy,' whispered Arabella to Rosemary, who also looked tired, after the midnight feast. 'I hope Mam'zelle doesn't pick on me if she wants to be cross. I hope she'll pick Elizabeth. Won't it be fun if she *does* start sneezing!'

There was oral French for the first ten minutes. Then Mam'zelle told the class to get out their French reading books. Elizabeth got out hers and opened it.

It was not long before the sneezing powder did its work. As the little girl turned over the pages, some of the fine white powder flew up her nose and tickled it. She felt a sneeze coming and got out her hanky.

'A-tish-oo!' she said. Mam'zelle took no notice.

'*A-tish-oo!*' said Elizabeth, wondering if she had got a cold. 'A-TISH-OOOOOO!'

Mam'zelle looked up. Elizabeth hastily tried to smother the next sneeze. There was a pause, in which Jenny read out loud from her French book. She came to the end of the page, and turned over. Everyone did the same.

The turning of the page sent more of the powder up Elizabeth's nose. She felt another sneeze coming and hurriedly put up her hanky. But she couldn't stop it.

'A-TISH-OOOO! A-TISH-OOOO!' The sneezes were quite loud enough to drown Jenny's reading. One or two of the children began to choke back giggles. They waited for Elizabeth's next sneeze. It came. It was such a loud one that it made Mam'zelle jump.

'Enough, Elizabeth,' she said. 'You will sneeze no more. It is not necessary. Do not disturb the class like this.'

'I can't – *a-tish-ooo* – help it,' said poor Elizabeth, with tears streaming down her cheeks, for the powder was very strong. 'A-tish-tish-tish-oooo!'

Mam'zelle became angry. 'Elizabeth! Last week it was drops falling on your head – this week it is sneezes. I will not have it.'

'A-tish-ish-ish-ooo-ooo,' said poor Elizabeth. The class began to laugh helplessly. Mam'zelle flew into a temper and banged on the desk.

'Elizabeth! You are a monitor and you behave like this! I will not have it. You will stop this sneezing game at once.'

'A-tish-OOOOOO!' said Elizabeth. The children laughed till the tears ran down their cheeks. This was the funniest thing they had ever seen.

'Leave the room, and do not come back,' ordered Mam'zelle sternly. 'I will not have you in my class.'

'But oh, Mam'zelle, please – tishoo, tishoo – tishoo – oh Mam'zelle,' began Elizabeth. But Mam'zelle came over to her, took her firmly by the shoulders, and walked her to the door.

She shut it behind Elizabeth and turned to face the class sternly.

'This is not funny,' she said. 'Not at all funny.'

The boys and girls thought it was. They tried their hardest to swallow down their giggles, but every now and again someone would choke, and that would set the whole class giggling again.

Mam'zelle was very angry indeed. She set them a page of poetry to copy out that evening as a punishment, but even that did not make the class stop giggling.

Elizabeth stood outside the door, upset and puzzled. 'Whatever made me sneeze like that?' she wondered. 'I'm not sneezing at all, out here. Am I starting a very bad cold? I simply could *not* stop sneezing in the classroom. It was mean of Mam'zelle to send me out here.'

And then, to Elizabeth's horror, William, the head-boy, came along, talking to Mr Lewis, the music-master. Elizabeth tried to look as if she wasn't there at all. But it was no use. William knew at once she had been sent out of the room.

'Elizabeth!' he said. 'Surely you haven't been sent out

of the room *again*! Rita told me you had, last week. Are you forgetting you are a monitor?'

'No,' said Elizabeth miserably. 'I'm not. Mam'zelle sent me out because I couldn't stop sneezing, William. She thought I was doing it on purpose. But I wasn't.'

'Well, you are not sneezing now,' said William.

'I know. I stopped as soon as I came out here,' said Elizabeth.

William walked on, thinking that Elizabeth must have been playing a silly joke. He would have to speak to Rita about it. They could not have monitors being sent out of the room like that. It was not right to have monitors setting a bad example.

Elizabeth had no idea that Julian had played a joke on her. She really thought she had been sneezing because she was beginning a cold. She was surprised when no cold came.

'Well, I shall go to the Meeting tonight,' she thought. 'And it will serve Julian right to be shown up in front of everyone. I know they will believe me, because I am a monitor.'

CHAPTER FIFTEEN

A stormy Meeting

THE CHILDREN filed into the big hall for the usual School Meeting that night. Elizabeth was excited and strung-up. She longed to get the Meeting over, and have everything settled.

'Any money for the Box?' said William, as usual. Ten pounds came in from a boy who had had a postal order from an uncle. Arabella put in two pounds – her birthday money. She had learnt her lesson about that! She was not going to be reported for keeping back money again.

Two pounds was given to everyone. Then William and Rita dealt with requests for more money. Elizabeth could hardly keep still. She felt nervous. She glanced at Julian. He sat as usual on the bench, a lock of hair falling into his eyes. He brushed it back impatiently.

'Any complaints?' The familiar question came from William, and a small boy sprang up before Elizabeth could speak.

'Please, William! The other children in my class are always calling me a dunce because I'm bottom. It isn't fair.'

'Have you spoken to your monitor about it?' asked William.

'Yes,' said the small boy.

'Who is your monitor?' asked William.

A bigger boy stood up. 'I am,' he said. 'Yes – the others do tease James. He has missed a lot of school through illness, so he doesn't know as much as the others. But I spoke to his teacher, and she says he could really try harder than he does, because he has good brains. He doesn't need to be bottom very long.'

'Thank you,' said William. The monitor sat down.

'Well, James, you heard what your monitor said. You yourself can soon stop the others teasing you, by using your good brains and not being bottom! You may have got so used always to being at the bottom that it didn't occur to you you could be anything else. But it seems that you can!'

'Oh,' said James, looking pleased and rather surprised. He sat down with a bump. His form looked at him, not quite knowing whether to be cross with him or amused. They suddenly nudged one another and grinned. James looked round, smiling too.

'Any more complaints?' asked Rita.

'Yes, Rita!' said Elizabeth, and jumped up so suddenly that she almost upset her chair. 'I have a very serious complaint to make.'

A ripple of whispering ran through the school. Everyone sat up straight. What was Elizabeth going to say? Arabella went rather pale. She hoped Elizabeth was not going to complain about *her* again. Julian glanced sharply at Elizabeth. Surely – surely she wasn't going to speak about him!

But she was, of course. She began to make her complaint, her words almost falling over one another.

'Rita, William! It's about Julian,' she began. 'I have thought for some time that he was taking things that didn't belong to him – and yesterday I caught him at it! I caught him with the things in his hand! He was taking them out of the old games locker in the passage.'

'Elizabeth, you must explain better,' said Rita, looking grave and serious. 'This is a terrible charge you are making. We shall have to go deeply into it, and unless you really have proof you had better say no more, but come to me and William afterwards.'

'I *have* got proof!' said Elizabeth. 'I saw Julian take the biscuits out of the locker. I don't know who they belonged to – Miss Ranger, I suppose. Anyway, Julian must have found them there, and when he thought we were all asleep at night he went to take them. And I heard him and saw him.'

The whole school was quite silent. The first-formers looked at one another, their hearts beating fast. Now their midnight feast would have to be found out! Julian would have to give away their secret.

William looked at Julian. He was sitting with his hands in his pockets, looking amused.

'Stand up, Julian, and tell us your side of the story,' said William.

Julian stood up, his hands still in his pockets. 'Take your hands out of your pockets,' ordered William. Julian did so. He looked untidy and careless as he stood there, his green eyes twinkling like a gnome's.

'I'm sorry, William,' he said, 'but I can't give any explanation, because I should give away a secret belonging to others. All I can say is – I was not stealing the biscuits. I was certainly *taking* them – but not stealing them!'

He sat down. Elizabeth jumped up, like a jack-in-the-box. 'You see, William!' she said, 'he can't give you a proper explanation!'

'Sit down, Elizabeth,' said William sternly. He looked at the first-formers, who all sat silent and uncomfortable, not daring to glance at one another. How good of Julian not to give them away! How awful all this was!

'First-formers,' said William gravely, 'I hope that if any one of you can help to clear Julian of this very serious charge, you will do so, whether it means giving away some secret or not. If Julian, out of loyalty to one or more of you, cannot stick up for himself, then you must be loyal to him, and tell what you know.'

There was a silence after this. Rosemary sat trembling, not daring to move. Belinda half got up then sat down again. Martin looked straight ahead, rather pale.

It was Arabella who gave the first form a great surprise. She suddenly stood up, and spoke in a low voice.

'William, I'd better say something, I think. We *did* have a secret, and it's decent of Julian not to give it away.

You see – it was my birthday yesterday – and we thought we'd have a – a – a midnight feast.'

She stopped, so nervous that she could hardly go on. The whole school was listening with the greatest interest.

'Go on,' said Rita gently.

'Well – well, you see, we had to hide the things here and there,' said Arabella. 'It was all such fun. We didn't tell Elizabeth – because she's a monitor and might have tried to stop us. Well, Julian hid my biscuits in the old games locker – and he went to get them after midnight, when the feast had begun. I suppose that's when Elizabeth means. But they were *my* biscuits, and I asked him to get them, and he brought them back to the common-room where we were. And I think it's unfair of Elizabeth to accuse Julian of stealing them. She's done that before. The whole form knows she's been saying that he takes money and sweets that don't belong to him.'

This was a very long speech. Arabella finished it suddenly, and sat down, almost panting. Julian looked at her gratefully. He knew that she would not at all like telling the secret of the midnight party – but she had done it to save him. His opinion of the vain little girl went up sky-high – and so did everyone else's.

William and Rita had listened closely to all that Arabella had said. So had Elizabeth. When she had heard the explanation of Julian's midnight wanderings she went very white, and her knees shook. She knew in a moment that in that one thing, at any rate, she had made a terrible mistake. William turned to Elizabeth, and his eyes were very sharp and stern.

'Elizabeth, it seems that you have done a most unforgivable thing – you have accused Julian publicly of something he hasn't done. I suppose you did not even ask him to explain his action to you, but just took it for granted that he was doing wrong.'

Elizabeth sat glued to her seat. She could not say a word.

'Arabella says that this is not the only time you have accused Julian. There have been other times too. As this last accusation of yours has been proved to be wrong, it is likely that the other complaints you have made to the first form are wrong too. So we will not hear them in public. But Rita and I will want you to come to us privately and explain everything.'

'Yes, William,' said Elizabeth in a low voice. 'I'm – I'm very, very sorry about what I said just now. I didn't know.'

'That isn't any excuse,' said William sternly. 'I can't think what has happened to you this term, Elizabeth. We made you a monitor at the end of last term because we all thought you should be – but this term you have let us all down. I am afraid that already many of us are thinking that you should no longer be a monitor.'

Several boys and girls agreed. They stamped on the floor with their feet.

'Twice you have been sent out of your classroom,' said

William. 'And for the same reason – disturbing the class by playing foolish tricks. That is not the behaviour of a monitor, Elizabeth. I am afraid that we can no longer ask you to help us as a monitor. You must step down and leave us to choose someone else in your place.'

This was too much for Elizabeth. She gave an enormous sob, jumped down from the platform and rushed out of the room. She was a failure. She was no good as a monitor. And oh, she had been *so* proud of it too!

William did not attempt to stop her rushing from the room. He looked gravely round the well-filled benches. 'We must now choose another monitor,' he said. 'Will you please begin thinking who will best take Elizabeth's place?'

The children sat still, thinking. The Meeting had been rather dreadful in some ways – but to every child there had come a great lesson. They must never, never accuse anyone of wrong-doing unless they were absolutely certain. Every child had clearly seen the misery that might have been caused, and they knew that Elizabeth's punishment was just.

Poor Elizabeth! Always rushing into trouble. What would she do now?

CHAPTER SIXTEEN

Elizabeth sees William and Rita

A NEW monitor was chosen in place of Elizabeth. It was a girl in the second form, called Susan. Not one child outside the first form had chosen a first-former. It was clear that most people felt that the first form would do better to have an older girl or boy for a monitor.

'Arabella, it *was* brave of you to own up about the midnight feast,' said Rosemary admiringly. All the others thought so too. Arabella felt pleased with herself. She really had done it unselfishly, and she was rather surprised at herself for doing such a thing. It was nice to feel that the rest of the form admired her for something.

One person was feeling rather uncomfortable. It was Julian. He felt very angry with Elizabeth for making such an untruthful and horrible complaint about him – but he did know that it was because of his tricks she had been sent out of the room twice, and not because of her own foolishness. Partly because of his tricks and their results, Elizabeth had lost the honour of being a monitor.

'Of course, William and Rita might have said she couldn't be because she complained wrongly about me,' said Julian to himself. 'But it sounded as if it was because of her being sent out of the room. Well, she doesn't deserve to be a monitor anyway – so why should I worry?'

But he did worry a little, because, like Elizabeth, he was really very fair-minded, and although he did not like the little girl, he knew that dislike was no excuse at all for being unfair. He had come very well out of the whole affair, thanks to Arabella. But Elizabeth had not. Even Harry, Robert, and Kathleen, her own good friends, had nothing nice to say of her at the moment.

The meeting broke up after choosing the new monitor. The children went out, talking over what had happened. You never knew what would come out at a School Meeting.

'Nothing can be hidden at Whyteleafe School!' said Eileen, one of the older girls. 'Sooner or later everyone's faults come to light, and are put right. Sooner or later our good points are seen and rewarded. And we do it all ourselves. It's very good for us, I think.'

Miss Belle and Miss Best had been present at the Meeting, and had listened with great interest to all that had happened. William and Rita stayed behind to have a word with them.

'Did we do right, Miss Belle?' asked William.

'I think so,' said Miss Belle, and Miss Best nodded too. 'But, William, have Elizabeth along as soon as ever you can, and let her get off her chest all that she has been thinking about Julian – there is clearly something puzzling there. Elizabeth does not get such fixed ideas into her head without *some* reason. There is still something we don't know.'

'Yes. We'll send for Elizabeth now,' said Rita. 'I wonder where she is.'

She was out in the stables in the dark, sobbing against the horse she rode each morning. The horse nuzzled up to her, wondering what was upsetting his little mistress. Soon she dried her eyes, and sat down on an upturned pail in a corner.

She was puzzled, deeply sorry for what she had said about Julian, very much ashamed of herself, and horrified at losing the honour of being a monitor. She felt that she could never face the others again. But she knew she would have to.

'What is the matter with me?' she wondered. 'I make up my mind to be so good and helpful and everything and then I go and do just the opposite! I lose my temper. I say dreadful things – and now everyone hates me. Especially Julian. It's funny about him. I did see that he had my marked pound. I did see that one of my sweets fell out of his pocket. So that's why I thought he was stealing the biscuits, and he wasn't. But did he take the other things?'

Someone came by calling loudly. 'Elizabeth! Where are you?'

Messengers had been sent to find her, to tell her to go to Rita and William. She could not be found in the school, so Nora had come outside to look for her with a torch.

At first Elizabeth thought she would not answer. She simply could not go in and face the others just yet. Then a little courage came to her, and she stood up.

'I'm not a coward,' she thought. 'William and Rita have punished me partly for something I *haven't* done – because I really *didn't* play about in class – but the other thing I *did* do – I did make an untruthful complaint about Julian, though I thought at the time it was true. So I must just face up to it and not be silly.'

'Elizabeth, are you out here?' came Nora's voice again.

This time the little girl answered. 'Yes. I'm coming.'

She came out of the stables, rubbing her eyes. Nora flashed her torch at her. 'I've been looking everywhere for you, idiot,' she said. 'William and Rita want you. Hurry up.'

'All right,' said Elizabeth, feeling her heart sink. Was she going to be scolded again? Wasn't it enough that she should have been disgraced in public without being scolded in private?

She rubbed her hanky over her face and ran to the school. She made her way to William's study. She knocked at the door.

'Come in!' said William's voice. She went in and saw the head-boy and girl sitting in arm-chairs. They both looked up gravely as she came in.

'Sit there,' said Rita in a kindly voice. She felt sorry for the headstrong little girl who was so often in trouble. Elizabeth felt glad to hear the kindness in Rita's voice. She sat down.

'Rita,' she said, 'I'm terribly sorry for being wrong about Julian. I did think I was right. I honestly did.'

'That's what we want to see you about,' said Rita. 'We couldn't allow you to say any more about Julian in public, in case you were wrong again. But we want you to tell us now all that has happened to make you feel so strongly against Julian.'

Elizabeth told the head-boy and girl everything – all

about Rosemary's money going and Arabella's; how her own marked pound had gone – and had appeared in Julian's hand, when he was spinning coins; and how her own sweet had fallen from his pocket.

'You are quite, quite sure about these things?' asked William, looking worried. It was quite clear to him that there *was* a thief about – somebody in the first form – but he was not so sure as Elizabeth that it was Julian! He and Rita both thought that whatever the boy's faults were, however careless and don't-careish he was, dishonesty was not one of his failings.

'So you see, William and Rita,' finished Elizabeth earnestly, 'because of all these things I jumped to the idea that Julian was stealing the biscuits last night. It was terribly wrong of me – but it was the other things that made me think it.'

'Elizabeth, why did you think you could put matters right yourself, when the money first began to disappear?' asked Rita. 'It was not your business. You should not have laid a trap. You should have come straight to us, and let us deal with it. You, as a monitor, should report these things to us, and let us think out the right way of dealing with them.'

'Oh,' said Elizabeth, surprised. 'Oh. I somehow thought that as I was a monitor I could settle things myself – and I thought it would be nice to put things right without worrying you or the Meeting.'

'Elizabeth, you must learn to see the difference between

big things and little things,' said Rita. 'Monitors can settle such matters as seeing that no one talks after lights out, giving advice in silly little quarrels, and things like that. But when a big thing crops up we expect our monitors to come to us and report it. See what you have done by trying to settle the matter yourself. You have brought a terrible complaint against Julian, you have made Arabella give away the secret she wanted to keep, and you have lost the honour of being made a monitor.'

'I felt so grand and important, being a monitor,' said Elizabeth, wiping away two tears that ran down her cheek.

'Yes – you felt *too* grand and important,' said Rita. 'So grand that you thought you could settle a matter that even Miss Belle and Miss Best might find difficult! Well, there is a lot you have to learn, Elizabeth – but you do make things as hard for yourself as possible, don't you!'

'Yes, I do,' said Elizabeth. 'I don't think enough. I just go rushing along, losing my temper – and my friends – and everything!' She gave a heavy sigh.

'Well,' said William, 'there is one thing about you, Elizabeth – you *have* got the courage to see your own faults, and that is the first step to curing them. Don't worry too much. You may get back all you have lost if only you are sensible.'

'I think we had better get Julian here and tell him all that Elizabeth has said,' said Rita. 'Perhaps he can throw some light on that marked pound – and the sweet. I feel certain he didn't take them.'

'Oh – let me go before he comes,' begged Elizabeth, who felt that Julian was the very last person she wanted to meet just then. She pictured his green eyes looking scornfully at her. No – she couldn't bear to meet him just then.

'No – you must stay and hear what he has to say,' said Rita firmly. 'If Julian didn't take these things, there is something peculiar about the matter. We must find out what it is.'

So Elizabeth had to sit in William's study, waiting for Julian to come. Oh dear, what a perfectly horrid day this was!

CHAPTER SEVENTEEN

Good at heart!

JULIAN CAME at once. He was surprised to see Elizabeth in the study too. He gave her a look, and then turned politely to William and Rita.

'Julian, we have heard a lot of puzzling things from Elizabeth,' said William. 'We are sure you have an explanation of them. Will you listen to me, whilst I tell you them – and then you can tell us what you think.'

Julian listened whilst William told all that Elizabeth had poured out to him and Rita. Julian looked surprised and puzzled.

'I see now why Elizabeth thought I was the thief,' he said. 'It did look very odd, I must say. Did I really have the marked pound? And did a sweet of Elizabeth's really fall out of my pocket? I heard something fall, but as the sweet wasn't mine, I didn't pick it up. I saw it on the floor, but I didn't even know it had fallen from my pocket. I certainly never put it there.'

'How did it get there then?' said Rita, puzzled.

'I believe I've got that pound now,' said Julian suddenly. He felt in his pockets and took out a brand-new coin. He looked at it closely. In one place a tiny black cross could still be seen. 'It's the same pound,' said Julian.

'That's the cross I marked,' said Elizabeth, pointing to it. Julian stared at it thoughtfully.

'You know, I'm sure, now I come to think of it, that I didn't have a bright new pound like this out of the Box that week,' he said. 'I'd have noticed it. I'm sure I got two old pounds. So someone must have put this new coin into my pocket – and taken out an old one. Why?'

'And someone must have put one of Elizabeth's sweets into your pocket too,' said William. 'Does any boy or girl dislike you very much, Julian?'

Julian thought hard. 'Well, no – except, of course, Elizabeth,' he said.

Elizabeth suddenly felt dreadfully upset when she heard this. All her dislike for Julian had gone, now that she felt, with Rita and William, that Julian hadn't taken the money or sweets, but that someone had played a horrible trick on him.

'Elizabeth just hates me,' said Julian, 'but I'm sure she wouldn't do a thing like that!'

'Oh, Julian – of course I wouldn't,' said poor Elizabeth, almost in tears again. 'Julian, I don't hate you. I'm more sorry than I can say about everything that has happened. I feel so ashamed of myself. I'm always doing things like this. You'll never forgive me, I know.'

Julian looked gravely at her out of his curious green eyes. 'I have forgiven you,' he said unexpectedly. 'I never bear malice. But I don't like you very much and I can't be good friends with you any more, Elizabeth. But there is something I'd like to own up to now.'

He turned to William and Rita. 'You said, at the Meeting, that Elizabeth had twice been sent out of the room for misbehaving herself,' he said. 'Well, it wasn't her fault.' He turned to Elizabeth. 'Elizabeth, I played a trick on you over those books. I put springs under the bottom ones and they fell over when the springs had untwisted themselves. And I stuck pellets on the ceiling just above your chair, so that drops fell on your head when the chemicals in them changed to water. And I put sneezing powder in the pages of your French book.'

William and Rita listened to all this in the greatest astonishment. They hardly knew what Julian was talking about. But Elizabeth, of course, knew very well indeed. She gaped at Julian in the greatest surprise.

Springs under her books! Pellets on the ceiling that turned to water! Sneezing powder in her books! The little girl could hardly believe her ears. She stared at Julian in amazement, quite forgetting her tears.

And then, very suddenly, she laughed. She couldn't help it. She thought of her books jumping off her desk in that peculiar manner. She thought of those puzzling drops of water splashing down – and that fit of sneezing. It all seemed to her very funny, even though it had brought her scoldings and punishments.

How she laughed. She threw back her head and roared. William, Rita, and Julian could not have been more surprised. They stared at the laughing girl, and then they began to laugh too. Elizabeth had a very infectious laugh that always made everyone else want to join in.

At last Elizabeth wiped her eyes and stopped. 'Oh, dear,' she said, 'I can't imagine how I could laugh like that when I felt so unhappy. But I couldn't help it, it all seemed so funny when I looked back and remembered what happened and how puzzled I was.'

Julian suddenly put out his hand and took Elizabeth's. 'You're a little sport,' he said. 'I never for one moment thought you'd laugh when I told you what I'd done to pay you out. I thought you might cry – or fly into a temper – or sulk – but I never thought you'd laugh. You're a real little sport, Elizabeth, and I like you all over again!'

'Oh,' said Elizabeth, hardly believing her ears. 'Oh, Julian! You *are* nice. But oh, what a funny thing to like me again just because I laughed.'

'It isn't really funny,' said William. 'People who can laugh like that, when the joke has been against them, are, as Julian says, good sports, and very lovable. That laugh of yours has made things a lot better, Elizabeth. Now we understand one another a good deal more.'

Julian squeezed Elizabeth's hand. 'I don't mind the silly things you said about me, and you don't mind the silly things I did against you,' he said. 'So we're quits and we can begin all over again. Will you be my friend?'

'Oh *yes,* Julian!' said Elizabeth happily. 'Yes, I'd love to. And I don't care if you make hail or snow fall on my head, or put any powder you like into my books now. Oh, I do feel happy again.'

William and Rita looked at one another and smiled. Elizabeth seemed to fall in and out of trouble as easily as a duck splashed in and out of water. She could be very foolish and do silly, hot-tempered, wrong things – but she was all right at heart.

'Well,' said William, 'we have cleared up a lot of things – but we still don't know who the real thief was – or is, for he or she may still be taking other things. We can only hope to find out soon, before any other trouble is made. By the way, Elizabeth, if your first accusation of Julian was made privately and secretly, as you said, how was it that all the first form knew? Surely you did not tell them yourself?'

'No, I didn't say a word,' said Elizabeth at once. 'I said I wouldn't, and I didn't.'

'Well, I didn't say anything,' said Julian. 'And yet the whole form knew and came to tell me about it.'

'Only one other person knew,' said Elizabeth, looking troubled. 'And that was Martin Follett. He was in the stables, Julian, whilst we were outside. He came out when you had walked off, and he offered me a pound in place of mine that had gone. I thought it was very nice of him. He promised not to say a word of what he had heard.'

'Well, he must have told pretty well everyone, the little sneak,' said Julian, who, for some reason, had never liked Martin as much as the others had. 'Anyway, it doesn't matter. Well – thanks, William and Rita, for having us along and making us see sense.'

He gave his sudden, goblin-like grin, and his green eyes shone. Elizabeth looked at him with a warm liking. How could she *ever* have thought that Julian would do a really mean thing? How awful she was! She never gave anyone a chance.

'He's always saying he does as he likes, and he's not going to bother to work if he doesn't want to, and he doesn't care what trouble he gets into, and he plays the most awful tricks – but I'm certain as certain could be that he's good at heart,' said Elizabeth to herself.

And Julian grinned at her and thought: 'She flies into the most awful tempers, and says the silliest things, and makes enemies right and left – but I'm certain as certain can be that she's good at heart!'

'Well, goodnight, you two troublemakers,' said William, and he gave them a friendly push. 'Elizabeth, I'm sorry about you not being a monitor any more, but I think you see yourself that you want to get a bit more common sense before the children will trust you again. You do fly off the handle so when you get an idea into your head.'

'Yes, I know,' said Elizabeth. 'I've failed this time but I'll have another shot and do it properly, you see if I don't!'

The two went out, and William and Rita looked at one another.

'Good stuff in both those kids,' said William. 'Let's make some cocoa, Rita. It's getting late. Golly, I wonder who's the nasty little thief in the first form. It must be somebody there. He's not only a nasty little thief, but somebody very double-faced, trying to make someone else bear the blame for his own misdeeds by putting the marked pound into Julian's pocket!'

'Yes, it must be someone really bad at heart,' said Rita. 'Someone it will be very dffficult to deal with. It might be a girl or a boy – I wonder which.'

Julian and Elizabeth went down the passage to their own common-room. It was almost time for bed. There was about a quarter of an hour left.

'I'm coming into the common-room with you,' said Julian, and Elizabeth squeezed his arm gratefully. He had sensed that she did not want to appear alone in front of all the first form. It was going to be hard to face everyone, now that she had been disgraced, and was no longer a monitor.

'Thank you, Julian,' she said, and opened the door to go in.

CHAPTER EIGHTEEN

Julian is very funny

THE FIRST-FORMERS had been talking about Elizabeth most of the time, wondering where she was, and saying that it served her right to be punished. Everyone was on Julian's side, there was no doubt about that.

'I shall tell Julian just what I think of Elizabeth,' said Arabella. 'I never did like her, not even when I stayed with her in the hols.'

'I must say I think it was a pity that Elizabeth accused Julian without being certain,' said Jenny.

'I suppose she was feeling annoyed because she had been left out of my party,' said Arabella spitefully. 'So she got back at Julian like that.'

'No. That wouldn't be like Elizabeth,' said Robert. 'She does do silly things, but she isn't spiteful.'

'Well, I shan't speak a word to her!' said Martin. 'I think she's been mean to Julian.'

'Sh. Here she comes,' suddenly said Belinda. The door opened, and Elizabeth came in. She expected to see scornful looks and even to hear scornful words, and she did. Some of the children turned their backs on her.

Close behind her came Julian. He saw at once that the

first-formers were going to make things difficult for Elizabeth.

'Julian,' said Arabella, turning towards him. 'We all feel sorry to think of what you had to face at the Meeting tonight. It was too bad.'

'You must feel very sorry about it,' said Martin. '*I* should.'

'I did,' said Julian in his deep and pleasant voice, 'but I don't now. Come on, Elizabeth – we've still got about ten minutes before bed-time. I'll play a game of double-patience with you. Where are the cards?'

'In my locker,' said Elizabeth gratefully. It had been dreadful coming into the room and facing everyone – but how good it was to have Julian sticking up for her like this – her friend once more. She fumbled about for the cards in her locker.

Every boy and girl stared in the greatest astonishment at Julian. Had he gone mad? Was he being friendly to the person, the very person, who had said such awful things about him? It was impossible. It couldn't be true.

But clearly it was true. Julian dealt the cards, and soon he and Elizabeth were in the middle of the game. The others were so surprised that they watched silently, not finding a word to say. Arabella was the most surprised, and it was she who found her tongue first.

'Well!' she said, 'what's come over you, Julian? Don't you know that Elizabeth is your worst enemy?'

'You're wrong, Arabella,' said Julian in an amiable

voice. 'She's my best friend. Everything was a silly mistake.'

There was something in Julian's voice that warned the others to say nothing. They turned to their own games, and left Julian and Elizabeth alone.

'Thanks, Julian,' whispered Elizabeth.

His green eyes looked at her with amusement. 'That's all right,' he said. 'Count on me if you want any help, Worst Enemy!'

'Oh, Julian!' said Elizabeth, half laughing and half crying. Then the bell went for bed-time and everyone cleared away books and games and went upstairs.

Things were not very easy for Elizabeth the next few days. The other children did not forgive and forget as easily as Julian did, and they treated her coldly. One or two were nice to her – Kathleen was, and Robert, and Harry. But most of them took no notice of her, and seemed to be glad she was no longer monitor.

Joan, of the second form, who had been Elizabeth's friend in the first term, came to find her. She took Elizabeth's hand and squeezed it. 'I don't quite know the rights and wrongs of it all,' she said, 'but I do know this, Elizabeth – that you wouldn't have said what you did if you hadn't really thought it was true. It will all blow over and you'll be made monitor again, you'll see!'

Elizabeth was glad of the kind words that her real friends gave her. 'Now I know what it is like when people are kind to others in trouble,' she thought. 'I shall remember how much I like kindness now, when things have gone wrong – and I shall be the same to others if *they* get into trouble.'

Elizabeth looked very serious these days. She worked very hard, was very quiet, and her merry laugh did not sound nearly so often. Julian teased her about it.

'You've gone all quiet, like Rosemary,' he said. 'Come on – laugh a bit, Elizabeth. I don't want a gloomy friend.' But Elizabeth had had a shock and needed to get over it. Julian wondered what he could do to make her her old happy self. He began to think out a few jokes.

He told the children what he was going to do. 'Listen,' he said, 'when Mr Leslie, the science-master, takes us for science in the laboratory, I shall make some of my noises. But none of you must make out that you hear them. See? Pretend that you hear nothing, and we'll have a bit of fun.'

Science was a bit dull that term. Mr Leslie was rather boring, and very strict. The children did not like him much, so they looked forward with the greatest glee to Julian's idea. They rushed to the lab that morning with much eagerness.

'What noises will you make?' asked Belinda.

'Wait and see,' said Julian, grinning. 'We will have a bit of fun – and Mr Leslie will get a few surprises.'

He certainly did. He walked stiffly into the room, nodded to the children, and told them to take their places.

'Now, this morning,' he said, 'we are going to test potato slices for starch. I have here . . .'

He went on talking for a while, and then handed out small slices of potato. Soon all the children's heads were bent over their experiment.

A curious noise gradually made itself heard. It was like a very high whistle, so high that it might have been the continual squeak of a bat, or of a bow drawn over a very highly strung violin-string.

'Eeeeeeeeee,' went the noise. 'Eeeeeeeeee.'

All the boys and girls stole a look at Julian. He was bending over his work, and there was not a single movement of mouth, lips, or throat to be seen. Yet they all knew he must be making that weird noise.

Mr Leslie looked up sharply. 'What is that noise!' he asked at once.

'Noise?' said Jenny, with an innocent stare. 'What noise, Mr Leslie?'

'That high, squeaking noise,' said Mr Leslie impatiently.

Jenny put her head on one side like a bird, pretending to listen. All the other children did the same. From outside the window there came the sound of an aeroplane in the sky, and in a moment the plane came in sight.

'Oh. It was the aeroplane you heard, Mr Leslie,' said Jenny brightly. Everyone giggled.

Mr Leslie frowned. 'Don't be absurd, Jenny. Aeroplanes do not make a high, squeaking noise. There it is again!'

'Eeeeeeeeeee!' Everyone heard the noise, but pretended

not to. They bent their heads over their work, badly wanting to giggle.

Julian changed his noise. Into the room came a deep, growling noise. Mr Leslie looked startled.

'Is there a dog in the room?' he asked.

'A dog, Mr Leslie?' said Belinda, looking all round. 'I can't see one.'

Elizabeth exploded into a giggle which she tried to turn into a cough. The growling noise went on, sometimes hardly to be heard, sometimes very loud. Mr Leslie couldn't understand it.

'Can't you hear that noise?' he said to the nearest children. 'Like a growl.'

'You said it was a squeak just now, sir,' said Harry, looking surprised. 'Is it a squeaky growl, or a growly squeak?'

Elizabeth exploded again, and Jenny stuffed her hanky into her mouth. Mr Leslie grew very cross.

'There is nothing funny to laugh at,' he snapped. 'My goodness – what's that now?'

Julian had changed his noise, and a curious, muffled boom-boom-boom sound could be heard. It did not seem to come from anywhere particular, least of all from Julian!

Mr Leslie felt scared. He glanced at the children. Not one of them seemed to be hearing this new boom-boom noise. How strange! It must be his ears going wrong. He put his hands up to them. Perhaps he wasn't well. People had noises in their ears then.

Boom-boom-boom went the strange muffled sound. 'Can you hear a boom-boom noise?' said Mr Leslie in a low voice to Harry. Harry put his head on one side and listened. He listened with his hand behind one ear. He listened with it behind the other. He listened with both hands behind both ears.

Elizabeth gave a loud giggle. She really couldn't help it. Jenny giggled too. Mr Leslie glared at them. Then he turned to Harry.

'Well, if you can't hear it, it must be something wrong with my ears,' he said. 'Get on with your work, everyone. Stop giggling, Jenny.'

The next noise was like a creaking gate. It was too much for poor Mr Leslie. Muttering something about not feeling very well, he fled out of the classroom, telling the children to get on with their work till he came back.

Get on with their work? That was quite impossible! Peals of laughter, roars of mirth, squeals and giggles filled the room from end to end. Tears poured down Jenny's cheeks. Harry rolled on the floor, holding his aching sides. Elizabeth sent out peal after peal of infectious laughter. Julian stood in the middle of it and grinned.

'Oh, that *has* done me good!' said Elizabeth, wiping the tears from her eyes. 'I've never laughed so much in my life. Oh, Julian, you're marvellous! You *must* do it again. Oh, it was gorgeous!'

It did everyone good. Those gusts of laughter had cleared the air of all spitefulness, scorn, and enmity.

Everyone suddenly felt friendly and warm. It was good to be together to laugh and to play, to be friends. The first form was suddenly a much nicer place altogether!

CHAPTER NINETEEN

Julian has some shocks

JULIAN'S SUCCESS in Mr Leslie's class rather went to his head. He tried several other noises in Mam'zelle's class, and in the art class too. He tried a mooing noise in Mam'zelle's class, not knowing how terrified she was of cows.

Poor Mam'zelle honestly thought that a cow was wandering about in the passage outside, and she stood trembling in horror. 'A cow!' she said. 'It is nothing but a cow that makes that noise.'

'Moo-ooo,' said the cow, and Mam'zelle shuddered. She could not bear cows, and would never go into a field where there was one.

'I'll go and shoo the cow away, Mam'zelle,' said Jenny, enjoying herself. She rushed to the door and there began a great shooing, mooing noise which sent the class into fits of laughter. Then Mam'zelle suddenly came to the conclusion that cows do not usually wander about school passages, and she looked sharply at Julian. Could that dreadful boy be making one of his famous noises?

The first form had a wonderful time with Julian's noises and tricks. There seemed no end to them. His brilliant brains invented trick after trick, and they were so clever that no mistress or master seemed able to guess that they were tricks until it was too late.

Julian used the sneezing powder again, this time on Mr Lewis, the music-master, when he was taking a singing lesson. He took two or three forms together for singing, and the lesson quickly became a gale of laughter as poor Mr Lewis sneezed time after time, trying in vain to stop himself. Julian was quite a hero in the school for his many extraordinary jokes and tricks.

But he was not a hero to the teachers. They often talked of him, sometimes angrily, sometimes sadly.

'He's the cleverest boy we've ever had at Whyteleafe,' said Miss Ranger. 'Far and away the cleverest. If only he would work he would win every scholarship there is. His brains are marvellous if only he would use them.'

'He thinks of nothing but jokes,' said Mr Leslie angrily. He was now firmly convinced that the extra-ordinary noises he had heard in the science lesson had been made by Julian, and he was angry every time he thought of it. And yet that boy, as if to make up for playing such a trick, had written out a really brilliant essay for Mr Leslie, an essay that he himself would have been proud to write. He was an odd fellow, there was no doubt about it.

At the School Meeting following the one in which Elizabeth had lost her position as monitor, the little girl, now no longer on the platform with the 'Jury', but down in the hall with the others, had got up to speak.

'I just want to say that I know now I was completely wrong about Julian,' she said humbly. 'I have said so to him, and he has been very nice about it – and we are good friends again, so that shows you how nice he has been. I'm sorry I was such a bad monitor. If ever I am a monitor again I will do better.'

'Thank you, Elizabeth,' said William, as the little girl sat down. 'We are very glad to have Julian absolutely cleared of the charge against him – and glad to know that he has been big enough to forgive you and to be friends so quickly.'

There was a pause. Julian grinned at Elizabeth, and she smiled back. It was good to be friends once more. Then William spoke again, and a graver note was in his voice.

'But I have something else to say to Julian,' he said. 'Something not quite so pleasant, Julian. All your teachers are displeased with you. It is not so much that you play the fool in class, and play tricks and jokes, but that you only use your brains for those things and for nothing else. According to everyone you have really wonderful brains, inventive and original – brains that could do something for the world later on – but you only use them for nonsense and rubbish, and never for worthwhile work.'

He stopped. Julian flushed and put his hands deeper into his pockets. He didn't like this at all.

'It's all very well to keep your class in fits of laughter,

and to be a hero because of your jokes,' said William, 'but it would be much better to work hard also, and later on become a hero in the world of science, or in the world of inventions.'

'Oh, I don't care whether I'm famous or not when I'm grown-up,' said Julian rather rudely. He was always rude when he felt awkward. 'I just want to have a good time, do what I like and let others do what *they* like. Hard work is silly, and—'

'Stand up when you speak to us, and take your hands out of your pockets,' said William.

Julian frowned, stood up, and took his hands out of his pockets.

'Sorry, William,' he said, his green eyes looking rather angry. 'I haven't any more to say – only that they're *my* brains, and I can choose how to use them myself, thank you. All this goody-goody talk doesn't mean a thing to me.'

'I can see that,' said William. 'It's a pity. It seems you only care for yourself and what you want yourself. One day you will learn differently – but what will teach you, I don't know. I am afraid it will be something that will hurt you badly.'

Julian sat down, still red. Use his brains for hard work when he could have a good time and laze around, playing tricks and jokes to make his friends laugh! No, thank you. Time enough to use his brains when he had to go out into the world and earn his living.

Elizabeth said nothing to him about William's talk. It was a little like she herself had once said to him when she was a monitor. It wasn't goody-goody talk. It was common sense. Julian was silly not to work. He could win marvellous scholarships, and do all kinds of fine things when he grew up. It was odd that he didn't want to.

The only effect that William's talk had on Julian was to make him even lower in the form than before! He was nearly always bottom, but the next week his marks were so poor that even Julian himself was surprised when they were read out. He grinned round cheerfully. *He* didn't care if he was bottom or not!

The week went on, and soon half-term came near. The children began to talk about their parents coming to see them. Elizabeth spoke to Julian about it.

'Will your parents come, Julian?'

'I hope so,' said the boy. 'I'd like you to see my mother. She's simply lovely. She really is – and so pretty and merry and sweet.'

Julian's eyes shone as he spoke of his mother. It was clear that he loved her better than anything on earth. He loved his father too, but it was his pretty, happy mother who had his heart.

'It's because of Mother I wear my hair too long,' he said to Elizabeth with a laugh. 'She likes this silly haircut of mine, with this annoying lock of hair always tumbling over my forehead. So I keep it like that to please her. And she loves my jokes and tricks and noises.'

'But isn't she disappointed when she knows you are always bottom of the form?' asked Elizabeth curiously. 'My mother would be ashamed of me.'

'Oh, mine likes me to have a good time,' said Julian. 'She doesn't mind about places in class, or whether I'm top of exams or not.'

Elizabeth thought that Julian's mother must be rather odd. But then Julian was odd too – very lovable and exciting, but odd.

Half-term came at last – and with it came most of the children's parents, eager to see them. Mrs Allen came and Elizabeth gave her a great hug.

'You're looking well, darling,' said Mrs Allen. 'Now, we must ask Arabella to come with us, mustn't we – because no one is here to see her.'

'Oh,' said Elizabeth, '*must* we, Mother?'

She caught sight of Julian, and called to him. 'Julian, here's my mother. Has yours come yet?'

'No,' said Julian, looking a little worried. 'She hasn't – and she said she would be here early. I wonder if the car has broken down.'

Just then the telephone bell rang loudly in the hall. Mr Johns went to answer it. He beckoned to Julian and took the boy into the nearest room. Elizabeth wondered if anything had happened.

'Mother, I must just wait for Julian to come out before I go and get ready to come with you,' she said. She hadn't

long to wait. The door opened, and Julian came out. But what a different Julian!

His face was quite white, and his eyes were full of such pain that Elizabeth could hardly bear to look at them. She ran to him.

'Julian! What's the matter? What has happened?'

'Go away,' said Julian, pushing her away blindly, as if he could hardly see. He went into the garden by himself. Elizabeth ran after Mr Johns.

'Mr Johns! Mr Johns! What's the matter with Julian? Please – please tell me.'

'It's his mother,' said Mr Johns, 'she's very ill – desperately ill. His father is a doctor, you know, and he is with her, and some other very clever doctors too. She is too ill for him even to see her. It's rather a blow for him, as you can see. Maybe you can help him, Elizabeth. You're his friend, aren't you?'

'Yes,' said Elizabeth, all her warm heart longing to comfort the boy. He was so proud of his mother – he loved her so much. She was the most wonderful person on earth to him. Oh, surely, surely she would get better!

She ran to her mother. 'Mother, listen. I can't come out today. I'm so sorry – but Julian's mother is desperately ill – and I'm his friend, so I must stay with him. Could you just take Arabella out, do you think? I think I really must stay with Julian.'

'Very well,' said her mother, and she went to find Arabella. Elizabeth herself went to hunt for Julian.

Goodness knew where he would hide himself. He would be like a wounded animal, going to some hole. Poor, poor Julian – what could she say to comfort him?

CHAPTER TWENTY

Julian makes a solemn promise

JULIAN WAS nowhere to be seen. Wherever had he gone? Elizabeth called to Harry. 'Harry! have you seen Julian anywhere?'

'Yes – I saw him tearing down to the gates,' said Harry. 'What's the matter with him?'

Elizabeth didn't answer. She rushed down to the big school gates too. She wondered if Julian had thought of catching a train and going to his mother. She ran out of the gates and stood looking down the road.

Some distance away, hurrying fast, was a boy. It must be Julian. Elizabeth tore after him, panting. She must get hold of him somehow. He was in trouble, and she might be able to help him.

She ran down the country lane and turned the corner. There was no one in sight. How could Julian have gone so far in such a short time! He couldn't possibly have turned the next corner yet! Elizabeth hurried along, feeling worried.

She came to the next corner. There was no one in sight on the main road either. Where could Julian have gone? She went back some way, thinking that he might have gone into a field through a gate a little way back. She passed a red telephone kiosk without thinking of looking inside it – and she was very startled when she suddenly heard the click of the kiosk door, and heard Julian's voice calling her urgently.

'Elizabeth! Oh, Elizabeth! Have you got any change on you?'

Elizabeth turned, and saw that Julian was in the telephone-box. She ran to him eagerly, fumbling in her pocket for her money.

'Yes – here is a fifty pence – and some tens,' she said. 'What are you doing?'

'Telephoning my father,' said Julian. 'Mr Johns said I wasn't to, at school – he said my father wouldn't want to be worried by phone calls – and I dare say he's right – but I've *got* to ask him a few questions myself. But I haven't got the right money to put in the box for the call.'

He took the money Elizabeth offered, and shut himself in the telephone-box again. Elizabeth waited outside. She had to wait for a long time.

It was a quarter of an hour before Julian could get through to his father, and the boy was almost in despair with the delay. He kept brushing his long lock of hair back, and he looked so white and forlorn that it was all Elizabeth could do not to open the kiosk door and go in beside him.

But at last he got through to his father, and Elizabeth could see him asking urgent questions, though she could hear nothing. He spoke to his father for about five minutes, and then put down the receiver. He came out, looking very white.

'I think I'm going to be sick,' he said and went pale green. He took Elizabeth's hand, and went through the nearby gate into the field. He sat down, still looking green. But he wasn't sick. He slowly lost his green look, and a little colour came back to his cheeks.

'I'm an idiot,' he said to Elizabeth, not looking at her, 'but I can't help it. Nobody knows how much I love my mother – or how sweet and loving she is.'

Elizabeth saw that he was making a great effort not to cry, and she wanted to cry herself. She didn't know what to do or say. There didn't seem any words that were any use at all. So she just sat close to Julian and squeezed his hand.

At last she spoke in a low voice. 'What did your father say?'

'He said – he said – Mother had just got a tiny chance,' said Julian, and he bit his lip hard. 'Only a tiny chance. I can't bear to think of it, Elizabeth.'

'Julian – doctors are so clever nowadays,' said Elizabeth. 'She will get better. They'll do something to save her – you'll see!'

'My father said they're trying a new drug, a new medicine on her,' said Julian restlessly, pulling up the grass that grew beside him. 'He said that he and two other doctors have been working on it for years – and it's almost ready. He's getting some today, to try it on Mother. He says it's the last hope – it will give her a tiny chance.'

'Julian, your father must be very clever,' said Elizabeth. 'Oh, Julian, it must be marvellous to be as clever as that, and to be able to discover things that can save people's lives. Fancy – just fancy – if your father's clever work should save your mother's life. You must take after him in brains, I think, Julian. You're very clever too. Oh, Julian, one day *you* might be able to save the life of someone you love by using a great invention of your own.'

Elizabeth had said these words in order to comfort Julian – but to her dismay and horror the boy turned over on to the grass and began to sob.

'What's the matter? Don't do that,' begged Elizabeth. But Julian took no notice. After a while he sat up again, looked for a hanky which he hadn't got, and rubbed his hands over his dirty face. Elizabeth offered him her hanky. He took it and wiped his face.

'If my father's new drug *does* save my mother's life, it will be because of his years of hard work, it will be because he's used his brains to the utmost,' said Julian, almost as if he were speaking to himself. 'I thought he was silly to work so hard as he did, and hardly ever have a good time or take long holidays.'

He rubbed his eyes again. Elizabeth listened, not daring to interrupt. Julian was terribly in earnest. This was perhaps the biggest moment in his life – the moment when he decided which road he was going to tread – the easy, happy-go-lucky road, or the hard, tiring road his father had taken – the road of hard work, of unselfish labour, always for others.

Julian went on speaking, still as if he were thinking aloud.

'*I've* been given brains too – and I've wasted them. I deserve to have this happen to me. There's my father using his brains all these years – and maybe he can save my mother because of that. It's the finest reward he could have. Oh, if only I could still have my mother, how hard I'd work! It's a punishment for me. William said something would teach me sooner or later – and it might be something that would hurt me badly.' Julian brushed back his hair, and bit his trembling lip.

'You have got the most wonderful brain, Ju,' said Elizabeth in a low voice. 'I've heard the teachers talking about you. They said you could do anything you liked, anything in the world. And, you know, I do think if you've got a gift of any sort, or good brains, you can be very, very happy using them, and you can bring happiness to other people too. This isn't goody-goody talk, Julian, really it isn't.'

'I know,' said Julian. 'It's wise and sensible talk. Oh, why didn't I show Mother what I could do, when I had the chance? She would have been so proud of me! She always said she didn't mind what I did, or how I fooled about – but she would have been so proud if I'd really *done* something. Now it's too late.'

'It isn't – it isn't,' said Elizabeth. 'You know your

mother has a chance. Your father said so. Anyway, whatever happens, Julian, you can still work hard and use your brains and do something in the world. You could be anything you liked!'

'I shall be a surgeon,' said Julian, his green eyes gleaming. 'I shall find new ways of curing ill people. I shall make experiments, and discover things that will give millions of people their health again.'

'You will, Julian, you will!' said Elizabeth. 'I know you will.'

'But Mother won't be there to see me,' said Julian, and he got up suddenly and went to the gate. 'Oh, Elizabeth, I see why this has happened to me now. It's about the only thing that could have made me really see myself, and be ashamed. I wish – oh I wish . . .'

He stopped. Elizabeth knew what he wished. He wished that such a dreadful lesson need not have come to him. But things happened like that. The little girl got up and went through the gate with him.

They walked back to the school, and on the way they passed a small country church. The door was open.

'I'm going in for a minute,' said Julian. 'I've got a very solemn promise to make, and I'd better make it here. It's a promise that's going to last all my life. You stay outside, Elizabeth.'

He went inside the little, dim church. Elizabeth sat down on the wooden bench outside, looking at the early daffodils blowing in the wind.

'I'd better pray too,' she thought. 'If only Julian's mother would get better! But I don't somehow think she will. I think poor Julian will have to work hard and do brilliantly without his mother to be proud of him, and love him for his big promise.'

After a short while Julian came out again, looking more at peace. He had a very steadfast look in his green eyes, and Elizabeth knew that, whatever happened, his promise of a minute ago would never be broken. Julian's brains would no longer be used only to amuse himself. Now, all his life long, he would do as his father had done, and use them for other people. Perhaps, as he had said, he would be a great surgeon, a wonderful doctor.

They walked back to the school in silence. There were no boys or girls there, for they all had gone out with friends or parents. Julian gave Elizabeth back her dirty hanky.

'Sorry you've had to miss your outing,' he said with a crooked little smile, 'but I couldn't have done without you.'

'Let's take some food and go for a picnic,' said Elizabeth.

Julian shook his head. 'No,' he said, 'I want to be here – in case there's any news. There may not be, today, my father said – or even for a day or two. But there might be, you see.'

'Yes,' said Elizabeth. 'All right, we'll stay here. Let's go and do some gardening. John won't be there, but I know what to do. There are some lettuces to plant, and there is still a bit of digging to be done. Could you do that, do you think?'

Julian nodded. They went out together, and were soon working in the wind and the sun. How good it was to work in the wind and the sun! How good it was to have a friend, and stick by him in times of trouble!

CHAPTER TWENTY-ONE

Martin gives Elizabeth a surprise

NO NEWS came for Julian that day, except a message to say that his mother was about the same, no worse and no better. The other children were upset to hear of the boy's trouble, and everyone did their best to comfort him, in their various ways.

Strangely enough, Martin seemed the most upset. This was odd, Elizabeth thought, because Julian had never liked Martin very much, and had not troubled to hide it. Martin went to Elizabeth, looking very distressed.

'Can I do anything to help Julian?' he said. 'Isn't there anything I can do?'

'I don't think so,' said Elizabeth. 'It's kind of you to want to help, Martin – but even I can't do very much, you know.'

'Do you think his mother will get better?' asked Martin.

'I don't somehow think so,' said Elizabeth. 'It's going to be awful for him when the news comes. I wouldn't bother him at all if I were you, Martin.'

Martin shuffled about, fidgeting with books and pencils, and Elizabeth grew impatient.

'What's the matter with you, Martin? You are awfully fidgety!' she said. 'You keep shaking the table, and I want to write.'

There was only one person in the common-room besides Elizabeth and Martin, and that was Belinda. She finished what she was doing, and then went out. Martin shut the door and came back to Elizabeth.

'I want to ask your advice about something, Elizabeth,' he said nervously.

'Well, don't,' said Elizabeth at once. 'I'm not a monitor any more. I'm not the right person to ask for advice now. You go to our new monitor. She's sensible.'

'I don't know Susan, and I do know you,' said Martin. 'There's something worrying me awfully, Elizabeth – and now that Julian is in trouble, it's worrying me still more. I love my own mother very much too, so I know what Julian must be feeling. Please let me tell you what I want to, Elizabeth.'

'Martin, don't tell me,' said Elizabeth. 'Honestly, I shan't be able to help you. I'm not sure of myself any more – I keep doing the wrong things. Look how I accused poor Julian of stealing. I shall be ashamed of that all my life. He was so decent about it too. You go and tell Susan.'

'I can't tell someone I don't know,' said Martin in despair. 'I don't want you to help me. I just want to get it off my chest.'

'All right – tell me,' said Elizabeth. 'Have you done something wrong? For goodness' sake stop shuffling about, Martin. Whatever's the matter with you?'

Martin sat down at the table, and put his face in his hands. Elizabeth saw that his face was getting red, and

MARTIN GIVES ELIZABETH A SURPRISE

she wondered curiously what was up with him. He spoke in a muffled voice through his fingers.

'I took that money – quite a lot of it – from Arabella – and Rosemary – and you – and other people too. And I took the sweets and the chocolate – and I took biscuits too and cake once,' said Martin, in a funny dull voice.

Elizabeth sat staring at him, startled and shocked.

'You thief!' she said. 'You horrid, beastly thief. And yet you always seemed so kind and generous. Why, you even offered me a pound in place of the one I lost – and all the time *you* had taken it! And you offered Rosemary money too, and she liked you awfully for it. Martin Follett, you are a very wicked boy, and a horrid pretender too, because you made yourself out to be so kind and generous and all the time you were a deceitful thief.'

Martin said nothing. He just sat there with his face in his hands. Elizabeth felt angry and disgusted.

'What did you tell *me* for? I didn't want to hear. I accused poor, unhappy Julian of doing what *you* did, you beast. And oh, Martin – was it *you* who put the marked pound into Julian's pocket – and the sweet too – to make me think it was he who had taken them? Could you be so mean as that?'

Martin nodded. His face was still hidden. 'Yes. I did all that. I was afraid when I found that pound was marked – and I never liked Julian because he didn't like me. I was afraid that if I was found out, none of you would like me.

And I so badly wanted to be liked. Hardly anyone ever likes me.'

'I don't wonder,' said Elizabeth scornfully. 'Good gracious! It was mean enough to take the money and the other things – but it was much, much meaner to try and put the blame on somebody else. That's not only mean, but cowardly. I can't imagine why you've told me all this. It's a thing to tell William and Rita, not me.'

'I can't,' said Martin with a groan.

'Think of all the damage you've done!' said Elizabeth, growing very angry as she thought of it. 'You made me think poor Julian stole – and I accused him – and he got back at me by getting me turned out of class – and I lost my position as monitor. Martin Follett, I think you're the nastiest, most hateful boy I've ever met. I wish to goodness you hadn't told me.'

'Well – I can't bear to think that I got Julian into trouble, now that he's so – so desperately unhappy,' said Martin. 'That's why I told you. I had to get it off my chest. It seemed about the only thing I could do for Julian.'

'Well, I wish you'd confessed to somebody else,' said Elizabeth, getting up. 'I can't help you and I don't want to. You're mean and cowardly and horrible. You oughtn't to be at Whyteleafe. You're not fit to be. Anyway, I'm too worried about Julian just now to bother my head about *you*!'

The little girl gave Martin a scornful glance, got up and went out of the room. How disgusting! Fancy behaving like that – stealing, and then putting the blame on to others – and letting them bear it too!

Rosemary went into the common-room as Elizabeth walked out. Elizabeth went to a music-room, got out her music, and began to practise, thinking of Julian and Martin and herself, as she played.

After a short while the door of the practice-room opened and Rosemary looked in. Her pretty, weak little face looked rather scared as Elizabeth frowned at her. But for once in a way Rosemary was strong, and in spite of Elizabeth's frown she went into the music-room and shut the door.

'What do you want?' said Elizabeth.

'What's the matter with Martin?' asked Rosemary. 'Is he ill? He looked awful when I went into the common-room just now.'

'Good,' said Elizabeth, beginning to play again. 'Serves him right!'

'Why?' asked Rosemary in surprise.

Elizabeth would not tell her. 'I don't like Martin,' she said, and went on playing.

'But Elizabeth, why not?' said Rosemary. 'He's really awfully kind. You know, he's always giving away sweets and things. And if ever anyone loses their money, he offers to give them some. I really think he's the most generous boy I know. He never eats any sweets himself – he only keeps them to give away. I think he's most unselfish.'

'Go away, Rosemary, please. I'm practising,' said

Elizabeth, who didn't want to hear Martin praised just then.

'But, Elizabeth, what *is* the matter with poor Martin?' said Rosemary, overcoming her timidity for once. 'He really did look dreadful. Have you been saying anything unkind to him. You know how unkind you were to poor Julian. You never give anyone a chance, do you?'

Elizabeth did not answer, and Rosemary went out of the room, going so far as to bang the door because she really felt cross with Elizabeth. She did not like to go back to Martin because he had turned his back on her, and told her to go away. It was all very puzzling.

'I suppose Elizabeth has quarrelled with *him* now!' she thought. 'Well – I haven't done any good by going to her.'

But she had. As soon as she had gone, Elizabeth began to remember the things that Rosemary had said about Martin – and they suddenly seemed very strange to her.

'She said he was the most generous boy she knew,' said Elizabeth to herself. 'She said he never ate sweets himself but always gave them away. And when anyone loses their money he always offers them some. And it's quite true he offered *me* sweets and money. How odd to steal things and then give them away! I've never heard of that before.'

Elizabeth stopped practising, and began to think hard. How could Martin be mean and yet generous? How could he make people unhappy by taking their things, and make others happy by giving them things? It didn't seem to make sense. And yet he did – there was no doubt about it.

'He doesn't steal for himself,' thought Elizabeth. 'I do think it's odd. I wish I could ask someone about it. But I'm not going to Susan, and I'm certainly not going to William and Rita again just now. I don't want them to think I'm interfering again – and anyway I'm not a monitor now. It was tiresome of Martin to tell me.'

She thought about it all for some time, and then something happened that made her forget. It was in the middle of the arithmetic class.

The children heard the telephone bell ring shrilly in the hall. It rang two or three times and then someone went to answer it. Then footsteps came down the passage, and a knock came at the classroom door.

A maid came in and spoke to Miss Ranger. 'If you please, Miss, there's someone urgently wanting Master Julian on the telephone. It's a long-distance call, so I didn't go to tell Miss Belle, in case the call was cut off before Master Julian got to the phone.'

Julian was out of his seat almost before the maid had finished. With a face as white as a sheet he half ran out of the room and down the hall. Elizabeth's heart almost stopped beating. At last news had come for Julian. But was it good or bad? The whole class was silent, waiting.

'Let the news be good – let the news be good,' said Elizabeth to herself over and over again, and didn't even notice that she had made blots all across her book.

CHAPTER TWENTY-TWO

Martin really is a puzzle!

THERE CAME the faint tinkle of the telephone bell as the receiver was put down. Then came the sound of footsteps down the passage, back to the schoolroom – hurrying footsteps. The door was flung open, and Julian came in, a radiant Julian, with sparkling eyes and a smiling mouth.

'It's all right,' he said. 'It's good news. It's all right.'

'Hurrah!' said Elizabeth, most absurdly wanting to cry. She banged on her desk for joy.

'Good, oh good!' cried Jenny.

'I'm so glad!' shouted Harry, and he drummed with his feet on the floor. It seemed as if the children had to make some sort of noise to express their delight. Some of them clapped. Jenny smacked Belinda hard on the back, she didn't know why. Everyone was full of joy.

'I'm very glad for you, Julian,' said Miss Ranger. 'It has been a great worry. Now it's over. Is your mother much better?'

'Much – much better,' said Julian, his face glowing. 'And it was all because of that wonderful new medicine my father and his two friends have been working on for so many years. It gave my mother a chance, just a chance

– and this morning she suddenly turned the corner, and she's going to be all right. Gosh – I don't know how I'm going to do any more lessons this morning!'

Miss Ranger laughed. 'Well – there are only five minutes left of this lesson before break. You had better all clear away your books and have five minutes' extra break, just to work off your high spirits. Everyone is glad for you, Julian!'

So the first form put away their books, chattering gaily, and rushed out into the garden early. The other forms were surprised to hear them playing there before the bell had gone. Elizabeth dragged Julian to a quiet corner.

'Julian, isn't it marvellous? Are you happy again now?'

'Happier than I've ever felt before,' said the boy. 'I feel as if I've been given another chance – one more chance to show my mother she's got someone to be proud of. I'm going to work now! I'm going to take all my exams with top marks, I'm going to win any scholarship I can, I'm going to take my medical exams as young as possible, I'm going to use my brains in a way they've never been used before!'

'You'll be top of the form in a week,' laughed Elizabeth. 'But, Julian, don't give up being funny, will you?'

'Well – I don't know about that,' said Julian. 'I'll perhaps think of jokes and tricks in my spare time – but I shan't waste my time or anybody else's now by being too silly. I'll see. I'm turning over a new leaf – going all goody-goody, like you wanted me to be!'

'No – I didn't want that,' said Elizabeth. 'I like good people, but not goody-goody. Save up some noises and jokes for us, Julian – you'll want a bit of rest from hard work sometimes!'

Julian laughed, and they went off to play with the others. The boy was quite mad with delight. All his fears were gone – his mother was better – he would see her again soon – there was time this term to work hard for her, and let her see what he could do.

For a time Elizabeth forgot about Martin. Then she noticed him now and again, looking, as Rosemary had said, very forlorn. He hung round Julian in an irritating way, and Julian, who didn't like him, had difficulty in shaking him off.

'Oh blow – I'd forgotten about Martin,' thought Elizabeth to herself. 'Well, I shan't tell Julian what he told me. He's so happy today and I won't let Martin's meanness spoil his day. Anyway, I've been ticked off enough for trying to manage things my own way. I shan't bother about this. I should only get into trouble again.'

So she tried not to think any more about Martin. But soon he stopped trying to hang round Julian and began to hang round Elizabeth instead. He seemed completely lost somehow. Elizabeth was glad when bed-time came and she could get rid of him.

The excitements of the day were a bit too much for Elizabeth. She lay in bed that night and could not get to sleep. She turned this way, she turned that way, she punched her pillow, she threw off her eiderdown, she pulled it on again – but she couldn't go to sleep, no matter what she did!

She began to think about the puzzle of Martin. Again and again she thought: 'How can a person be two different things at one and the same time? How can you be selfish and unselfish, mean and generous, kind and unkind? I wish I knew.'

She lay and remembered all the School Meetings she had been to. She thought of the odd things some children did, and how, when the reason for their actions was found, they could be cured.

'There was Harry – he was a cheat – but it was only because he was afraid of being bottom of the form and letting his father down,' thought Elizabeth. 'And there was Robert – he was a bully last term – but it was only because he had once been dreadfully jealous of his small brothers, so he got rid of his jealousy by being beastly to other small children. And there's me – I was awful, but I *am* better now, even though I've been in disgrace this term.'

She remembered the Big Book in which William and Rita wrote down the accounts of every School Meeting. In it were the stories of many bad or difficult children who, through many a year at Whyteleafe, had had their faults and wrong-doings shown up, discussed kindly and firmly, and, in the end, been helped to cure themselves.

'I don't believe there's any cure for Martin, anyway,' thought Elizabeth. 'I wonder if there's anything in

William's Big Book that would explain Martin's funny behaviour. I'd like to see. Oh dear, I wish it was morning, then I could go and see.'

The children were allowed to refer to 'William's Big Book', as they called it, when they liked. There was so much sound common sense in it.

'I'll go and read it now,' thought Elizabeth suddenly. 'I shall never go to sleep tonight. There won't be anyone about now, so I'll just pop on my dressing-gown, go down to the hall, and find the book. It will be something to do anyway.'

She put on her dressing-gown and slippers. She crept out of the dormitory, where everyone was sound asleep, and went downstairs to the hall. On the platform was a table, and in the drawer of the table the big book was kept.

Elizabeth had a torch with her, for she dared not switch on the light. She opened the drawer and took out the book. It was filled with writing – different writing, for three or four head-boys and head-girls had kept the book throughout the time that Whyteleafe School had been running.

Elizabeth dipped here and there. *She* was in the Book too – here it was, 'The Bold Bad Girl' – that was what Harry had called her two terms ago, when she was the Naughtiest Girl in the School. And here she was again, made a monitor because of fine behaviour – and oh dear, oh dear, here she was again, disgraced because of bad behaviour!

'Elizabeth Allen lost her position as monitor because she accused one of her form wrongly of stealing, and because her behaviour in class showed that she was unsuited to be a monitor,' she read in William's neat, small handwriting.

'I seem to appear in this Book rather a lot,' said Elizabeth. She turned to the beginning pages of the Book and read with interest of other children who had been good or bad, difficult or admirable – children who had left the school long ago. Then the story of a girl began to interest her. It seemed very much like Martin's story.

She read it through, then shut the Book and thought hard. 'What a peculiar story!' she thought. 'Very like Martin's really. That girl – Tessie – she took money too – but *she* didn't spend any of it on herself – she gave it away as fast as she stole it. And she took flowers from the school garden, pretended she had bought them, and gave them to the teachers. And it was all because nobody ever liked her, so she tried to buy their liking and their friendship by giving them things. She stole so that she might appear kind and generous. I do wonder if Martin does the same.'

She went back to her bed, thinking. 'How awful to be so friendless that you've got to do something like that to get friends,' she thought. 'I wonder if I'd better say something to Martin tomorrow. He did look pretty miserable today. Anyway, I've had enough with interfering with other people. I'll just ask him a few questions, and then leave it. He can do what he likes about himself. I don't care.'

She went to sleep after that, and was so tired in the morning that she could hardly wake up. She went yawning down to breakfast, grinned at Julian, and sat down to eat her porridge. What had she been worrying about the night before? Her French? No – she knew that all right, thank goodness. Julian? No – that worry was gone now.

Of course – it was Martin she had been thinking about. She took a look at his pale face, and thought that he looked rather small and thin.

'He's a horrid boy,' she thought. 'Really horrid. Nobody *really* likes him, not even Rosemary, though they say he's kind and all that. It's funny he hasn't a single real friend. Horrid as I have sometimes been, I've always had real friends – somebody has always liked me.'

A chance came for Elizabeth to speak to Martin soon after breakfast. Elizabeth had rabbits to feed, and Martin had a guinea-pig. The cages were side by side and the two children were soon busy.

'Martin,' said Elizabeth, going straight to the point, as she always did. 'Martin, why do you give away the sweets and money and things you steal, instead of keeping them for yourself? Why steal them if you don't want them?'

'Only because I want people to like me, and you can't make people like you unless you're kind and generous,' said Martin in a low voice. 'My mother has always told me that. It's not *really* stealing, Elizabeth – don't say that

– I give the things away at once. It's – it's the same sort of thing that Robin Hood did.'

'No, it isn't,' said Elizabeth. 'Not a bit. It's stealing, and you know it is. How can you bear to know that you are so dishonest and mean, Martin? I should die of shame!'

'Well, I feel as if I'm dying of shame too, ever since you called me all those awful names yesterday,' said Martin in a trembling voice. 'I simply don't know what to do!'

'There's only one thing to do – and a little coward like you would never do it,' said Elizabeth. 'You ought to own up at the next Meeting that you took the things, and say that you put the blame on Julian! *That's* what you ought to do!'

CHAPTER TWENTY-THREE

A school match and other things

SCHOOL WENT happily on. A lacrosse match was played, and Elizabeth was in it. It was a home match, not an away match, so the whole school turned out to watch. Elizabeth felt most excited.

Julian was playing in the match too, and so was Robert. Julian was good at all games. He could run swiftly and catch deftly.

'We ought to put up a good show today,' said Eileen, when she took the team out on to the field. 'We've got some strong first-form players this term. Now, Elizabeth, keep your head, pass when you can, and for goodness' sake don't go up in smoke if one of your enemies kicks you on the ankle! Julian, keep by Elizabeth if you can, and let her pass to you. You catch better than anyone else.'

It was an exciting match. The other school had brought a strong team, and the two schools were very evenly matched. Elizabeth got a whack on the hand from someone else's lacrosse stick, that gave her so much pain she thought she would have to go off the field.

Julian saw her screwed-up face. 'Bad luck!' he called. 'You're doing well, Elizabeth. Keep it up! We'll shoot a goal soon, see if we don't!'

Elizabeth grinned. The pain got better and she played well. The other school shot three goals, and Whyteleafe also shot three. The children who were looking on anxiously consulted their watches – only one minute more to go!

Then Elizabeth got the ball and tore for the goal. 'Pass, pass!' yelled Julian. 'There's someone behind you!'

Elizabeth threw the ball deftly to him, and he caught it. But another enemy was on him at once, trying to knock the ball out of his net. He passed it back quickly to Elizabeth. She saw yet another enemy coming to tackle her, and in despair she flung the ball hard at the goal.

It was a wild shot – but somehow or other it got there! It bounced on a tuft of grass, and just avoided the waiting lacrosse net of the goal-keeper. It rolled into the corner of the goal-net and lay still.

Whyteleafe School went quite mad. The whistle blew for Time, and the two teams trooped off the field. Julian gave Elizabeth such a thump on the back that she choked.

'Good for you, Elizabeth!' said Julian, beaming. 'Just in the nick of time. Jolly good!'

'Well – it was really a fluke,' said Elizabeth honestly. 'I couldn't see where I was throwing. I just threw wildly, and by a fluke it went into the goal!'

The first-formers crowded round her, cheering her and patting her on the back. It was very pleasant. Then the two teams went in and had a most enormous tea. It was all great fun.

'I think you ought to be a monitor all over again!' said Rosemary. 'I never felt so thrilled and proud in my life as when you shot that last goal, Elizabeth, just as the whistle blew. I almost forgot to breathe!'

Elizabeth laughed. 'Golly – if people were made monitors just for shooting goals, how easy it would be!'

Nobody felt like doing prep that night. Julian longed to make a few noises. The others looked at him, trying to make him start something. Mr Leslie was taking prep and it would be fun to have a bit of excitement.

Julian wanted to please the others. He wondered what to do. Should he make a noise like a sewing-machine? Or what about a noise like bees humming?

He looked down at his book. He hadn't begun to learn his French yet. He remembered his promise, made so solemnly in the little country church a few days back. He was never going to forget that.

Julian put his hands over his ears and began to work. Maybe if there were a few minutes left at the end of prep he would do something funny – but he was going to do his work first!

Work was easy to Julian. He had a quick mind, and an unusual memory. He had already read a great deal, and knew a tremendous lot. He could easily beat the others if he tried. But it was not so easy to try at first, when he had let his mind be lazy for so long.

But at the end of the first week of trying, Julian was top of the form! He was one mark ahead of Elizabeth, who was also trying hard. Everyone was amazed, especially Miss Ranger.

'Julian, it seems that you must either be top or bottom,' she said, when she read out the marks. 'Last week you were so far at the bottom that I am surprised there were any marks to read out at all. This week you are a mark ahead of Elizabeth, who has been working extremely well. I am proud of you both.'

Elizabeth flushed with pleasure. Julian looked as if he didn't care a rap, but Miss Ranger knew that was only a pose. Something had changed him, and he cared now – he wanted to use his brains for the right things, not only for silly jokes and tricks.

'I think perhaps his mother's illness must have had something to do with it,' thought Miss Ranger. 'I do hope this great change lasts! Julian is a joy to teach when he really works. I hope he won't be bottom again next week.'

But Julian would never be bottom again. He was going to keep that promise all his life. He was not going to waste his brains any more.

Only Martin did badly that week – even worse than Arabella usually did! He was right at the bottom and Miss Ranger spoke sharply to him.

'You can do better than this, Martin. You have not been bottom before. You seem very dreamy this week.'

Martin was not really dreamy. He was worried. He wished he had not told Elizabeth his secret now. She had said such hard things to him, things he couldn't forget.

And she hadn't helped him at all.

Miss Ranger had a few words to say to Arabella also. 'Arabella, I am getting tired of seeing you so low in form. You are one of the oldest – the very oldest in fact. I think if you gave a little more attention to your work and a little less to whether your hair is looking nice, or whether your collar is straight or your nails perfect, we might see a little better work.'

Arabella went red. She thought Miss Ranger was very unkind. 'She speaks more sharply to me than to anyone else in the form,' she complained to Rosemary.

This was quite true – but Miss Ranger knew that she could only get at thick-skinned Arabella by plain speaking. The vain little girl hated to feel small, hated to be scolded or put to shame in front of anyone. Whyteleafe School was very good for her. There was plenty of plain speaking there.

Arabella decided not to be bottom the next week. She stopped fussing about her hair and her dress – at least she stopped fussing in class.

'You'll soon be quite passably nice, Arabella,' said Robert, who hadn't much time for the vain little girl. 'I haven't heard you ask Rosemary once today if your hair is tidy. It's simply marvellous!'

And, for once in a way, Arabella laughed at the joke against herself, instead of sulking. Yes, she really was getting 'passably nice' in some ways!

The next School Meeting came. 'It won't last long,'

said Elizabeth to Julian. 'There won't be much business done at it, Julian. Let's slip out quickly afterwards and bag the little table in the common-room. I've got a big new jigsaw we can do.'

'Right,' said Julian.

But there was more 'business' to be done at that Meeting than Elizabeth thought, and there was no time for a jigsaw puzzle that night. It was all quite unexpected, and nobody was more surprised than Elizabeth when it happened.

The Meeting opened as usual. There was very little money to be put into the Box, though a few children had postal orders. Then the money was given out.

'Any requests?'

'Please, William,' said one small boy, Quentin, 'the cage I keep my guinea-pig in fell over yesterday, and one side of it broke in. Could I have the money for another cage?'

'Well, that's rather expensive,' said William. 'There isn't a great deal of money in the Box at the moment. Can't you mend the cage?'

'I have tried – but I'm not very good at it,' said Quentin. 'I thought I'd done it all right, but I hadn't, and my guinea-pig got out. I was late for school because I had to catch it. It's in with Martin's guinea-pig now, but they fight.'

'I'll mend it for Quentin,' said Julian, actually remembering to stand up and take his hands out of his pockets. 'It won't take me long.'

'Thank you, Julian,' said William. 'There really isn't a great deal of money in the Box at the moment. But I believe there are quite a lot of birthdays next week, so maybe we shall have a full Box again soon. Any more requests?'

Nobody quite liked to ask for any more money as there wasn't much to spare.

'Any complaints?' said William. There was a dead silence. It was clear there were none.

'Well, there's nothing much to say this week – except that I am sure the whole school will like to know that Julian is top of his form, instead of bottom, this week,' said William with a sudden smile. 'Keep it up, Julian!'

'That is the nice part about Whyteleafe School,' thought Elizabeth. 'You get blamed – but you do get praised too, and that's lovely!'

'You may go,' said William, and the children got up to go. But, in the middle of the noise of feet, there came a voice.

'Please, William! I've got something to say!'

'Sit down again,' ordered William, and everyone sat in surprise. Who had spoken? Only one boy was on his feet – and that was Martin Follett, looking very green and shaky. 'What do you want to say, Martin?' asked William. 'Speak up!'

CHAPTER TWENTY-FOUR

Martin gets a chance

ELIZABETH LOOKED in astonishment at Martin. Surely he could not be going to tell his own secret – that it was he who had stolen the money and tried to put the blame on to Julian!

'He's such a mean, deceitful, horrid boy,' she thought, 'and a real coward. Whatever is he going to say?'

Martin swallowed once or twice. He seemed to find it difficult to say a word now. William saw that he was dreadfully nervous and he spoke more kindly to him.

'What is it you want to say, Martin? Don't be afraid of saying it. We are always ready to hear anything at the School Meeting, as you know.'

'Yes. I know,' said Martin in rather a loud voice, as if he was trying to get all his courage together at once. 'I know. Well – I took that money – and all the other things – and I put that pound into Julian's pocket, and the sweet too, so that nobody would think it was me – they would think it was Julian.'

He stopped speaking, but he didn't sit down. Nobody said a word. Martin suddenly spoke again. 'I know it's awful. I dare say I'd never have owned up except for two things. I couldn't bear it when Julian's mother was ill – I mean, it was awful to think I'd done a mean trick to someone who was miserable. And the other thing that made me speak was – someone said I was a coward, and I'm not.'

'You certainly are not,' said Rita. 'It is a courageous thing to do – to stand up and confess to something mean. But why did you steal, Martin?'

'I don't really know,' said Martin. 'I know there's no excuse.'

Elizabeth had sat and listened to all this in the greatest surprise. Fancy Martin being brave enough to say all that in front of everyone! Now Julian was completely cleared of any blame. She looked at Martin and felt suddenly sorry for him.

'He so badly wanted people to like him, and they don't,' she thought, 'and now he has had to own up to something that will make them dislike him all the more! Well – that was a brave thing to do.'

William and Rita were talking to one another. So were the monitors. What was to be done with Martin? How was this to be tackled? Elizabeth suddenly remembered what she had read in the big Book the night before. She stood up.

'William! Rita! I understand about Martin! He hasn't got any excuse for what he did, but there's a real reason, it wasn't just badness. It wasn't the usual sort of stealing.'

'What do you mean, Elizabeth?' asked William, in surprise. 'Stealing is always stealing.'

'Yes, I know,' said Elizabeth, 'but Martin's sort was strange. He only took things from other people so that he might give them away! He never kept them himself.'

'Yes, that's quite true,' said Rosemary, most surprisingly forgetting her timidity, and standing up beside Elizabeth. 'He gave me money whenever I lost mine, and he is always giving away sweets. He never keeps any for himself.'

'William, there's a bit about the same sort of thing in our big Book – the one on the table in front of you,' said Elizabeth eagerly. 'I couldn't help wondering why Martin seemed such a funny person – you know, kind and unkind, mean and generous – it seemed so odd to be opposite things at once – and there's a bit about a girl in our Book who was just the same.'

'Where?' asked William, opening the Book. Elizabeth walked up to the platform, bent over the Book, turned the pages, and found the place. 'There you are!' she said, pointing.

'How did you know it was here?' asked Rita.

'Well – Martin told me all he'd done, and I was disgusted,' said Elizabeth, 'but I was also puzzled about him – and I wondered if there was anything about that kind of thing in our Book – so I looked, and there was.'

William read the piece and passed it to Rita. They spoke together. Elizabeth went back to her place. Martin was looking very miserable, wishing heartily that he had never said a word now. He felt that everyone's eyes were on him, and it was not at all a nice feeling.

William spoke again, and everyone listened intently. 'Stealing is always wrong,' said William, in his clear, pleasant voice. 'Always. People do it for many reasons – greed – envy – dishonesty. All bad reasons. But Martin did it for a different reason. He did it because he wanted to buy friendship. He did it because he wanted to buy people's liking and admiration.'

William paused. 'He took things in order to give them away to someone else. He may have thought to himself that because it is good to give to others, it was therefore not bad to take them away from someone else. But they were not his to give. It was stealing just the same.'

A tear trickled down Martin's cheek and fell on the floor. 'I want to go away from Whyteleafe,' he said in a low voice, without standing up. 'I shall never do any good here now. I've never done any good anywhere.'

'You can't run away like that,' said William. 'What's the good of trying to run away from yourself? You've got courage or you wouldn't have stood up and said what you did. We all make silly mistakes, we all have bad faults – but what really matters is – are we decent enough to try and put them right? You did have a reason for what you did, a silly reason. Now you see it was silly, and you see that what you did was bad. All right – that's the end of it.'

'What do you mean – that's the end of it!' said Martin in surprise.

'The end of your silly habit of taking what doesn't belong to you in order to buy friendship!' said William.

'You know quite well you *can't* buy it. People like you for what you are, not for what you give them. Well – if the reason for that bad habit is gone, the habit goes too, doesn't it? You'll never steal any more.'

'Well – I don't think I shall,' said Martin, and he sat up a little straighter. 'I've felt so guilty and so ashamed. I'll take another chance.'

'Good,' said William. 'Come and see me this evening and we'll get things a bit straighter. But I think you must pay back each week any money you have taken from different children, and you must also buy sweets to give back to those you took them from. That's only fair.'

'Yes, I will,' said Martin.

'And we'll give him a chance and be friendly,' suddenly said Elizabeth, eager to do her bit to help. How she had disliked Martin! Now she wanted to help him! What was there about Whyteleafe School that made you see things so differently all of a sudden? It was odd.

'It seems to me,' said Rita, in her slow distinct voice, 'it seems to me as if Elizabeth is a much better monitor when she isn't one than when she *is*!'

The children laughed loudly at this. Elizabeth smiled too. 'Rita is right,' she thought, surprised. 'I do seem to be wiser when I'm not a monitor than when I am! Oh, how topsy-turvy I am!'

The Meeting broke up at last. Martin went to Julian. 'I'm sorry, Julian,' he muttered, not looking at the boy at all.

'Look at me,' commanded Julian. 'Don't get into the habit of not looking at people when you speak to them, Martin. Look at me, and say you're sorry properly.'

Martin raised his eyes and looked rather fearfully into Julian's green ones, expecting to see scorn and anger. But he saw only friendliness there. And he said he was sorry properly.

'I am sorry. I was a beast. I've learnt my lesson and I'll never be two-faced again,' he said, looking straight into Julian's eyes.

'That's all right,' said Julian. 'I like you better now than I did before, if that's any comfort to you. Look, William is wanting you.'

Martin went off with William. What William said to him nobody ever heard, but Rosemary, who saw him coming from the study later, said that Martin looked much happier.

'I'm going to be really friendly to him,' she said. 'He'll want a friend. I never thought he was bad, I always thought he was nice. So I shall go on thinking it.'

Elizabeth looked in surprise at the timid Rosemary. Good gracious – that was another person changing! Who would have thought that Rosemary, who agreed with everyone, would say straight out that she was going to be friends with someone like Martin!

'You simply never know about people,' thought Elizabeth. 'You think because they're timid they'll always be timid, or because they're mean they'll always be mean. But they can change awfully quickly if they are treated right. Golly, Arabella will be changing and forget to be vain and boastful! No – that could never happen!'

There was no time to do the jigsaw – only just time to clear away the things left out, and have some supper and go to bed.

'Things do happen here, don't they?' said Julian, with a grin. 'Come on down to supper.'

At supper Miss Ranger was continually annoyed by the buzzing of a bluebottle. She looked all down the table for it, but could see it nowhere.

'Where *is* that fly?' she said. 'It's very early in the year for a bluebottle, surely! Kill it somebody. We can't have it laying eggs in our meat.'

The bluebottle buzzed violently, and Mr Leslie, at the next table, looked all round for it. It really was becoming a nuisance.

Elizabeth looked suddenly at Julian. He grinned at her and nodded. 'Oh – it's one of Julian's noises!' she thought, and exploded into a giggle. Then everyone knew – and how they laughed, even Miss Ranger.

'I thought it was a good time to play a joke,' said Julian when he said goodnight to Elizabeth. 'We had all had such a very serious evening. Goodnight, Elizzzzzzzzzzzzzabeth!'

CHAPTER TWENTY-FIVE

An adventure for Elizabeth

THE DAYS went swiftly by, days of work and play, riding and gardening, looking after pets, going for nature rambles – it was extraordinary the way the weeks flew by.

'Once the beginning of the term is past, the end seems to appear so quickly!' said Elizabeth. 'There doesn't seem to be much middle to a term!'

'Let's go for a nature walk this afternoon,' said Julian. 'We've got an hour and a half quite free. Don't garden with John – he's got plenty of helpers at the moment with that tribe of youngsters – we'll go over the hills and down to the lake.'

'All right,' said Elizabeth, looking out of the window at the brilliant April sunshine. 'It will be lovely on the hills – we might find primroses on our way.'

So, that afternoon, the two set off together. They carried nature-tins on their backs, for they meant to bring back many things for the nature class. 'We'll find frog-spawn in the lake,' said Julian. 'I bet there's plenty there, and tadpoles too.'

They went over the hills together. 'We must be back by tea-time,' said Elizabeth. 'That's the rule, unless we have permission to stay out later. My watch is right. I don't want to get into trouble again for anything just at present. I've not been too bad this last week or two!'

Julian grinned. He thought that of all the children in the form Elizabeth probably tried hardest to be good, and yet walked into trouble more often than anyone else. You never knew what was going to happen to Elizabeth.

'She seems to make things happen, somehow,' thought Julian. 'She's such a fierce little person, so downright and sincere. Well – we've both had our ups and downs this term. Let's hope we'll have a little peace till the end of term.'

They went over the hills, picking primroses in the more sheltered corners. The sun shone down quite fiercely, and Elizabeth took off her blazer and carried it.

'This is lovely,' she said. 'Julian, look, there's the lake. Isn't it beautiful?'

It was. It lay smooth and blue in the April sunshine. There seemed to be nobody there at all. The children were pleased to think they would have it all to themselves.

They began to look for frog-spawn. There was none to be found – but there were plenty of tadpoles. They caught some and put them into their jars.

'I feel a bit tired now,' said Elizabeth. 'Let's sit down.'

'I'm going up the hill a bit,' said Julian. 'I want to find some special sort of moss. You sit here and wait for me.'

Julian disappeared. After a while Elizabeth thought she heard him coming back – but it was someone else. It was a child of about six, nicely dressed, with big blue eyes and very red cheeks. He was panting as if he had been running.

Elizabeth was surprised to see him all alone. He seemed rather small to be allowed near the lake by himself. She lay back and shut her eyes, letting the sun soak into her.

She heard the little boy playing about – and then she heard a loud splash. At the same moment she heard a terrified scream, and she sat up suddenly.

The little boy had disappeared. But a little way out on the lake some ripples showed, and then a small hand was flung up.

'Golly! That boy has fallen in!' said Elizabeth in dismay. 'He must have crawled out on that low tree-branch, and tumbled off. I thought he oughtn't to be here by himself.'

Then a woman appeared, running. 'Where's Michael? Did I hear him scream?' she called anxiously. 'He ran away from me. Have you seen a little boy anywhere?'

'He has fallen into the water,' said Elizabeth. 'Can he swim?'

'No, oh no! Oh, he'll be drowned,' cried the woman. 'Oh, let's get help quickly.'

There was no help to be got. Elizabeth quickly undid her shoes. 'I'll wade in and get him,' she said. 'If the water is too deep, I'll have to swim.'

She waded out, feeling the sand of the lake-bottom just under her stockinged feet. Suddenly the sandy bottom fell away, and Elizabeth was out of her depth. She had to swim.

She was a good swimmer, and she struck out at once –

but it was not easy to swim in clothes. They weighed her down dreadfully. Still, she managed somehow, and it was only a few strokes that she had to swim. Her quick mind remembered all she had learnt about life-saving.

She caught hold of the sinking child and pulled him towards her. At once he clung to her, almost pulling her under too.

'Leave go!' ordered Elizabeth. 'Leave go! I will hold *you*, not you me.'

But the child was too frightened to leave go. He pulled poor Elizabeth right under, and she gasped and spluttered. Somehow she undid his arms from round her neck, turned him over on his back, put her hands under his armpits, and swam on her back to the shore, pulling the kicking child along.

Soon she felt the sandy bottom under her feet and she struggled to stand. The child slipped from her hands and went under again. He got caught in some weeds and did not float up to the top. Elizabeth was in despair. She went under the water herself to look for him, and caught sight of a leg. She got hold of it and pulled hard.

The child came out of the weeds. He was no longer struggling. 'Oh dear – I believe he is drowned,' thought Elizabeth in horror. She dragged him to the shore. He was quite limp, and lay still.

His nanny bent over him, moaning, and quite terrified. Elizabeth thought she was silly. 'Look, we must work his arms up and down, up and down, like this,' she said.

'That will bring air into his lungs and make him breathe again. Look – work his arms well.'

The girl was tired, and she let the nanny do the life-saving work, then she took her turn – and suddenly the child gave a big sigh and opened his eyes.

'Oh, he's alive – he's alive!' cried the nanny. 'Oh, Michael, Michael – why did you run away from me?'

'You'd better get him home as soon as he can walk,' said Elizabeth. 'He's wet through. He'll catch an awful chill.'

The nanny took the child off in her arms, weeping over him, forgetting even to say thank you to the little girl who had saved him. Elizabeth took off her dress and squeezed it dry. She began to shiver.

Suddenly Julian appeared down the hill. He stared in the greatest astonishment at Elizabeth. 'Whatever *have* you been doing?' he asked. 'You're wet through.'

'I had to pull a kid out of the water,' said Elizabeth. 'I couldn't help getting wet. I hope Matron won't be angry with me. Good thing I took my blazer off – I've got one dry thing to put on at any rate.'

'Come on home, quick,' said Julian, helping her on with her blazer. 'We're late anyway – and now you'll have to change all your clothes. Oh, Elizabeth – you can't even go out for a walk without doing something like this!'

'Well, I couldn't leave the child to drown, could I?' said Elizabeth. 'He ran away from his nanny.'

They went home as quickly as they could. The tea-bell

went as they reached the school. 'I'll slip in to tea and say you are coming in a minute,' said Julian. 'Hurry up.'

Elizabeth hurried up – but she was cold and shivery, and wet clothes are not easy to take off. She put them in the hot-air cupboard to dry hoping that Matron would not see them there before she herself had time to take them out.

'I don't see how I could help it, all the same,' said Elizabeth, drying herself on a towel. 'I just had to pull that child out of the water. I bet he would have drowned if I hadn't.'

Matron didn't notice the wet clothes. Elizabeth was able to take them out of the cupboard before she saw them. She had a sharp word from Miss Ranger for being late for tea, but otherwise it seemed as if things were all right.

'Oh, Julian – I left my jar of tadpoles by the lake,' said Elizabeth in dismay, after tea. 'Aren't I an idiot?'

'Well – you must share mine,' said Julian. 'I've got plenty. I suppose if you go about dashing into lakes rescuing silly kids, you are bound to forget something or other.'

Elizabeth laughed. 'Don't tell anyone, please,' she said. 'Matron doesn't know my clothes were wet, and the others would only tease me if they knew I'd dashed into the lake like that.'

So Julian said nothing. He hadn't seen Elizabeth swim to the child's rescue, he hadn't known what a hard task it had been to get him safely to shore, or how Elizabeth had brought him back from death by showing the nanny how to work his arms up and down to make him breathe again. He just thought she had waded into the water, slipped and got wet, and pulled the child out.

So nobody knew, and Elizabeth forgot about it. She was working very hard indeed, trying to keep pace with Julian, who, now that he was using his brains properly, seemed likely to beat her easily every single week.

'It's most annoying!' said Elizabeth, giving him a friendly punch. 'I do my best to make you use your brains and work hard – and what happens? I lose my place at the top of the form! I shall complain about you at the Meeting tonight, Julian. I shall say that you are robbing me of my rightful place at the top of the form. So be careful!'

'There'll be no excitement at the Meeting tonight, old thing,' said Julian. 'We've all been as good as gold lately.'

But he was wrong. There was plenty of excitement!

CHAPTER TWENTY-SIX

Happy ending

THE CHILDREN always enjoyed the weekly School Meetings, even if there was not much business to be done. It was good to meet all together, good to share their money, good to see their head-boy and girl on the platform, with the serious monitors near by.

'You feel how much you belong to the school then,' said Jenny. 'You really feel part of it, and you know that what you are and do really matters to the whole school. It's a nice feeling.'

There were only two weeks to go till the end of the term. No one had any money at all to put into the Box. But there had been several birthdays two or three weeks before, so there was still plenty of money to share.

It was given out as usual, and then William allowed ten pounds to go to John to buy two big new watering-cans.

'One of ours has two holes in it and they can't be mended,' said John. 'The water drips out on to our feet and wets them all the time. And the other can is so small. Last summer we lost a lot of plants because we didn't do enough watering, and this time I want plenty of water if the weather's dry. So I'd be awfully glad to have two new cans.'

The garden had looked lovely that early spring.

Crocuses had blazed on the school bank, daffodils were out everywhere, wallflowers were filling the air with their delicious scent, and polyanthus had flowered along the edges of the beds. John and his helpers had done really well. The whole school was willing to buy him cans, barrows, spades – anything he wanted. They were very proud of John and his hard work.

Nobody else wanted any money. There were no complaints either. It looked as if it was going to be a short and rather dull Meeting. But no – what was this? Miss Belle and Miss Best were actually walking up from the back of the big hall! *They* had something to say, they had business to discuss! Mr Johns came with them.

In surprise William and Rita gave them chairs, wondering what was happening. The school looked up to the platform, wondering too. It couldn't be anything awful, because Miss Belle and Miss Best were smiling.

The headmistresses sat down. Mr Johns sat beside them. They spoke a little and then Miss Belle got up.

'Children,' she said, 'it is not often that Miss Best, Mr Johns, and I come up here to speak to you at a School Meeting – unless, of course, you ask us. But this time we have something to say – something very pleasant – and I want to say it in front of the whole school.'

Everyone listened eagerly. Whatever could it be? Nobody had the least idea.

Miss Belle took a letter from her bag and opened it. 'I have had a letter,' she said. 'It is from a Colonel Helston, who lives not far from here. This is what he says.'

Miss Belle read the letter and everyone listened with interest and excitement.

'Dear Madam – Four days ago my little son, Michael, ran away from his nanny. He fell into the lake near your school, and would have been drowned if it had not been for a girl from Whyteleafe. This girl waded into the water, then swam to Michael. Michael struggled hard and pulled her under the water. She got him on his back, and swam towards the shore with him. He slipped from her hands and became entangled in some weeds. He was without any doubt drowning at that moment. The girl dived into the weeds and pulled him out. When she got him to shore she showed the nanny how to bring him back to life again, and herself helped to do this, with the result that he lived, and is now safe and well with me at home.

I was away at the time, and only came back today, to hear this amazing story. I do not know which girl it was. All I know is that the nanny saw she had a Whyteleafe school blazer on the ground near by, and I would like you, please, to tell me the name of the child so that I may thank her myself, and give her some reward for her very plucky action. She saved the life of my little boy – he is my only child – and I can never be grateful enough to the little girl from Whyteleafe School, whoever she may be. Yours sincerely,

Edward Helston.'

The children listened in amazement. Who could it be? Nobody knew. But then, whoever it was must have come home with wet clothes – surely they would have been seen. The children looked from one to the other. Julian nudged Elizabeth. His green eyes shone with pride in his friend. Elizabeth was as red as a beetroot. 'What a fuss about nothing!' she thought.

'Well,' said Miss Belle, folding up the letter, 'this surprising letter gave me and Miss Best very great pride and pleasure. We do not know who this girl is. We asked Matron if anyone had given her wet clothes to dry, but no one had. So it is a complete mystery.'

There was a silence. Elizabeth said nothing at all. Everyone waited.

'I should like to know who it is,' said Miss Belle. 'I should like to give her my heartiest congratulations on a brave deed that she said nothing about. The whole school should be proud of her.'

Elizabeth sat quite still. She simply could *not* stand up and say anything. For the first time in her life she really felt shy. She hadn't done anything much – only just pulled that child out of the water – oh dear, what a fuss about it all!

Julian got to his feet. 'It was Elizabeth!' he said, so loudly that it sounded almost like a shout. 'Of course it was Elizabeth! Who else could it be? It's exactly like her, isn't it? It was our Elizabeth!'

The children craned their necks to look at Elizabeth.

She sat on the floor, still very red, with Julian patting her on the shoulder.

Then the clapping and cheering began! It nearly brought the roof down. Elizabeth might be naughty and hot-tempered and often do silly, wrong things – but she was as sound and sweet as an apple in her character, and all the children knew it.

Clap, clap, clap, hurrah, hurrah, bang, bang, clap, clap! The noise went on for ages, until Miss Belle held up her hand. The sounds died down.

'Well – so it was Elizabeth!' she said. 'I might have guessed it. Things always happen to Elizabeth, don't they? Come up here on the platform, please, Elizabeth.'

Elizabeth went up, flaming red again. Miss Belle, Miss Best, and Mr Johns actually shook hands with her solemnly and said they were very proud of her.

'You are bringing honour to the name of Whyteleafe,' said Miss Belle, her eyes very bright. 'And you bring honour to yourself at the same time. We would like to give you a reward ourselves, Elizabeth, for your brave deed. Is there anything you would like?'

'Well . . .' said Elizabeth, and paused. 'Well . . .' she said again. Julian wondered what she was going to say. Was she going to ask if she might be made a monitor again?

'I'd like you to give the school a whole holiday, please,' said Elizabeth, in a rush, thinking that she

was asking rather a big thing. 'You see – there's a big fair on at the next town soon – and it would be such fun if you would give us a whole holiday, so that we could go to it. We've all been talking about it, and I know everyone would like to go. Do you think we could?'

There was another outburst of cheering and clapping. 'Good old Elizabeth!' shouted somebody. 'Trust her to ask something for the school, and not for herself!'

Miss Belle smiled and nodded. 'I think we might say yes to what Elizabeth wants, don't you?' she said, and Miss Best nodded too. Elizabeth smiled, very pleased. She might have been in great disgrace, and made the children think bad things of her that term – but anyway she had made up for it now by getting them a whole holiday to go to the fair.

She turned to go down into the hall again. But somebody was standing up, waiting to speak. It was Julian.

'What is it, Julian?' asked Miss Belle.

'I am speaking for the whole of the first form,' said Julian. 'We want to know if Elizabeth can be made a monitor again, now, this very night? We think *she* ought to have some reward. And we want her for our monitor. We all trust her and like her.'

'Yes, we do, we do!' cried Jenny, and a few others. Elizabeth's eyes shone like stars. How marvellous! To be made a monitor because the whole form wanted it, and wanted it so badly! Oh, things were wonderful!

'Wait, Elizabeth,' said Miss Belle, stretching out her hand and pulling the little girl to her. 'Do you want to be made a monitor again?'

'Oh yes, please,' said Elizabeth happily. 'I can do better now. I know I can. Let me try. I won't let anyone down again. I'll be sensible and wise, really I will.'

'Yes, I think you will,' said Miss Belle. 'We won't pass round bits of paper and vote for you, Elizabeth, as we usually do – you shall be monitor from this very minute. Susan shall still be monitor too. For once in a way we must have an extra one! A very special extra one!'

So Elizabeth went to sit at the monitor's table, proud and pleased. Everyone was glad, even Arabella. How could anyone not be glad, when Elizabeth had so generously asked for something for the whole school, instead of asking for something for herself alone, as she might so easily have done?

'Well, that was a good Meeting, wasn't it?' said Julian, when the children at last filed out of the hall, chattering and laughing in excitement. 'This has been a thrilling term, I must say. I'm glad I came to Whyteleafe School. It's the best school in the world!'

'Yes, it is,' said Elizabeth. 'Oh, I do feel so happy, Julian.'

'You've a right to,' said Julian. 'Funny person, aren't

you? Naughtiest girl in the school – and best girl in the school! Worst enemy – and best friend! Well, whichever you are, you're always Our Elizabeth, and we're proud of you!'